MANATEE SUMMER

MANATEE
SUMMER

Evan Griffith

Quill Tree Books
An Imprint of HarperCollinsPublishers

Quill Tree Books is an imprint of HarperCollins Publishers.

Manatee Summer
Copyright © 2022 by Evan Griffith
All rights reserved. Printed in Lithuania.
No part of this book may be used or reproduced in any manner
whatsoever without written permission except in the case of
brief quotations embodied in critical articles and reviews. For
information address HarperCollins Children's Books, a division of
HarperCollins Publishers, 195 Broadway, New York, NY 10007.
www.harpercollinschildrens.com

Library of Congress Control Number: 2021951496
ISBN 978-0-06-309491-8
Typography by Laura Mock
22 23 24 25 26   SB   10 9 8 7 6 5 4 3 2 1
❖
First Edition

For Arthur

MANATEE SUMMER

ONE

Papa's manatee story goes like this.

When he was a kid, way before he met Nana, and *way* before I even existed, he used to take his dad's canoe out into the Indigo River, hoping to catch some fish to fry. His family didn't have much money, so he wanted to help out. And one day, instead of fish, Papa found a manatee.

He gave up on fishing and followed the manatee down the river, away from town, into a cove ringed with palm trees. It was a cloudy day, but when the sun came out, Papa saw another manatee swimming near the canoe, and then another, and another, until he realized there was a whole herd of manatees in the cove.

Papa sat there for hours, till sunset, while the manatees puttered around his canoe. He says it was one of the most

1

magical days of his life. He says that sitting there, watching them, he felt peaceful—like he didn't have anywhere else to be. Like it didn't matter what happened yesterday or what might happen tomorrow. Like, for a little while at least, everything was okay.

I love the story, but I also love the way Papa tells it—the way he smiles his crooked smile and waggles his bushy eyebrows when he describes the manatees as big gray blobs. I love his voice, too. It's the deepest voice I've ever heard, like he's drawing it up from the bottom of the sea. Like each word is a sunken treasure.

But ever since Papa got a kind of dementia called Alzheimer's, his manatee story has been changing. He takes away certain parts and adds others. Now he says that he stayed with them past sunset, till the stars came out. He says that the manatees danced and somersaulted in the water. I don't know if I believe that bit about the somersaults, though.

Honestly, I don't know if I believe any of it anymore. I've never seen a cove ringed with palm trees, and I've biked a whole lot of the Indigo River coast. I've never seen a manatee, either, even though they're supposed to live in the river and I've been looking for them for basically my whole life, a.k.a. eleven years.

I want to believe Papa's story. I want to hold on to it. But it feels like trying to hold on to a wave at the beach, the way I did when I was little and didn't know any better.

I'd stand waist-deep in the ocean and dig my toes into the sand. When a wave reached the shore, I'd try to wrap my arms around it, but it always slipped away.

One time it even carried me with it. I lost my footing, and my whole world turned to water, and for a few seconds there was no up or down, no sky or sand, just me spinning in the darkness until Papa's hand found mine.

TWO

"There!" I say, pointing to a speckled lizard racing along the bank of the canal.

Tommy squats for a closer inspection. "Brown anole," he says. "Discovery #22." He pushes his glasses up the bridge of his nose. "Peter, I estimate there's a seventy-eight percent chance we've run out of lizard species native to central Florida."

I scowl. "You're a nonbeliever."

"But I believe in lots of things," says Tommy. "Like gravity. And chlorophyll."

"Chloro-what?"

"Chlorophyll. It's the pigment in plants that makes them green." He's talking fast now, the way he always does when he gets going about a new word he just learned. "I was

listening to a *Science Daily* podcast about the plant repro-
ductive cycle—"

"Good grief, Tommy," I say, sponging the sweat off my
face with my shirt.

It's the first day of summer vacation, and the sun must
know it, too, because it's *hot*. Even for Florida. It's one of
those days when your skin stings and the pavement looks
all blurry and it's so humid you feel like someone just
threw a big wet blanket over you. It's hard to get enough
oxygen, and you definitely don't want to breathe with your
mouth open, because there are about one gazillion mosquitos buzzing around your head, and the air is thick with
the smell of dead catfish wafting up from the Indigo River.

The road scorches my bare feet, so Tommy and I stick
to the grassy bank of the canal that runs into our neighborhood from the river. Well, *I* stick to the bank. Tommy
keeps his distance. He's been scared of water ever since
spring break, when he got caught in a rip current at the
beach and his dad, a risk analyst, told him there was a
7 percent chance he could've been swept right out to sea
and drowned.

"Sunscreen?" Tommy says, pulling a bottle out of one
of the pockets of his cargo shorts. "It's SPF 100. That's the
highest SPF."

I wave the bottle away. "You know I hate that stuff."

"But Peter, remember last summer when we were out

in the sun all day and you didn't wear sunscreen and you burned and then peeled for a whole week?"

"No," I say, even though I totally do remember. My skin aches just thinking about it.

While Tommy smears a thick coat of sunscreen on his arms and legs, I keep looking for animals. Our neighborhood curls like a horseshoe around the canal, and there are usually lots of birds and reptiles down here by the water. Tommy says the canal is like its own little ecosystem— another word he learned from *Science Daily.*

A sudden flash of red in the branches of an oak tree catches my eye.

"Binoculars!" I say.

Tommy scrambles to hand them over. I zoom in on the spot of red, then sigh. "Red-winged blackbird."

"Discovery #72," says Tommy, rubbing sunscreen on his cheeks.

The tricky thing about discoveries is that the more you make, the harder it is to make new ones. Still, this is it. This summer—our last summer before middle school— Tommy and I will finally finish our Discovery Journal. I know it. I can *feel* it. Three long months ahead of us and only six discoveries to go. If we just keep our eyes open—

"Well, well! School's out already?"

Shoot. I was so busy trying to make a discovery that I didn't notice Mr. Reilly standing on the dock in front of his ugly yellow house on the other side of the canal. My blood starts to boil, and it's not just the billion-degree heat. Mr. Reilly is my archnemesis.

"Y-Yes, sir," Tommy says, even though I've told him a thousand times to stop calling Mr. Reilly *sir*.

"And let me guess," says Mr. Reilly. "You boys are out here getting into some kind of trouble?"

He smirks at us from across the canal. With his big straw hat and string-bean arms, he looks like a scarecrow that somebody made the mistake of bringing to life. He's almost blocking the entire sun with his hat, which is a very Mr. Reilly thing to do.

I look from Mr. Reilly to his speedboat, the *Reckoner*, bobbing in the water at the end of his dock. He had the name custom-painted along the side in jagged red letters that are probably supposed to be edgy but are really just silly. Another very Mr. Reilly thing to do.

"Can't two kids go for a walk?" I growl.

Mr. Reilly shrugs his knobby shoulders and shifts his jaw from side to side. Mrs. Reilly made him give up chewing tobacco ages ago, but his mouth never learned how to stop chewing. "Depends where you're walking," he says.

I glare at Mr. Reilly, right into that face of old, sun-cracked leather, because I'm not afraid of him. I don't care that he won the lottery last year, or that he's the president of the Indigo River Boating Club, or that he's got a shiny

7

new speedboat. He's not some big shot to me. The day I met him, he yelled at me and Tommy for standing in his yard so we could see an eastern cottontail rabbit up close. Ever since, I've known exactly what he is—a bully.

A hundred insults are on the tip of my tongue—some of them are pretty creative, too—but then I think back to last summer when Mr. Reilly caught me and Tommy plucking avocados off the avocado trees in his backyard. Actually, he only caught *me* plucking avocados. He caught Tommy hiding behind his dumpster, waiting for me to finish. Anyway, he ratted me out to my mom and she grounded me for a whole week. So maybe I should try to not tick off Mr. Reilly this summer, even though ticking off Mr. Reilly is one of my specialties.

I guess Mr. Reilly is thinking back to that day, too. "I've counted every avocado on every avocado tree in my backyard," he says. "So I'll know if any go missing."

"You don't even use the avocados," I say. "You just let them fall and rot!"

Mr. Reilly frowns. "I made guacamole once." He squints at Tommy. "Your parents getting that porch screening replaced?"

"Yes, sir. I mean—" Tommy sneezes. "I think so, sir."

"Good," says Mr. Reilly, hopping down into the *Reckoner.* "Good, good, good."

I have no idea why Mr. Reilly and Tommy are talking

about porch screening, but I'm not sticking around to find out. "Come on, Tommy," I say. I don't have to say it twice. Tommy is always ready to run away from Mr. Reilly. Tommy is always ready to run away from *everything*.

But we've barely taken a single step before the engine of Mr. Reilly's speedboat roars to life and a shower of filthy river water is raining down on us as he takes off flying down the canal, going *way* faster than the 10-miles-per-hour canal speed limit.

While Tommy coughs and splutters, I start chasing after Mr. Reilly and the *Reckoner*, my fists clenched, my heart pounding. He's *not* getting away with this.

Or . . . maybe he is. He's already speeding out of the canal and into the Indigo River. I kick a stubby palm tree with my bare foot. It hurts. I say a word I'm not supposed to say but Mom says all the time.

"It's okay," says Tommy. "I mean, the Indigo River is full of bacteria and there's a ninety-three percent chance all those bacteria are now crawling around our skin and I have a very sensitive immune system, but—" Another sneeze. Tommy has seasonal allergies in every season. "But it's okay."

"It's *not* okay," I say. "Did the Discovery Journal get wet?"

Tommy peeks inside his backpack. "I think my body shielded it."

Well, that's a relief, at least.

I check my watch to make sure it's okay, too.

The watch was a birthday gift from Papa. He's given me lots of watches—he used to own a watch repair shop, before he got sick and moved in with me and Mom—but this one is the coolest. The clockface is a model of the solar system. The hour hand ends on Earth, the minute hand ends on Jupiter, and the second hand ends on Pluto, even though Pluto isn't a real planet. It's a dwarf planet, according to Tommy. Anyway, I've worn the watch every day since Papa gave it to me, and I have a feeling that I'm going to be checking it a lot more this summer now that I'm on Official Caregiver Duty.

The watch is a little wet, but Earth and Jupiter and Pluto are still circling the sun. And it's only two forty-five, so I don't have to go home just yet—Papa's next pill dose is at three o'clock. He's probably still asleep, anyway. Most days, he naps after lunch.

Tommy and I keep walking along the canal. I shake my head back and forth like a dog so the water flies out of my hair. Tommy tries to wipe his glasses clean, but he can't find a dry spot anywhere on his clothes. Then he starts stumbling around, the way he does whenever he can't see right. We sit down in the grass so he doesn't walk himself right into the canal. He sits a little farther back from the water than I do.

"There aren't any rip currents in canals, you know."

"I know," says Tommy. Still, he doesn't move any closer.

I could tell Tommy about the time I went to the beach with Papa and a wave pulled me under. It wasn't a rip current, but it was still pretty scary, like the ocean was swallowing me whole. Maybe Tommy would feel better if he knew he's not the only one who was almost swept out to sea.

But that was a long time ago. I was just a little kid. I'm not afraid of anything now. Not the ocean, and not Mr. Reilly, either.

"I *hate* that guy," I say, plucking a blade of grass and ripping it in half. "What's wrong with him?"

"He's a little disagreeable," says Tommy.

"Why don't you just call him a jerk?"

Tommy has always used big words—at least, he's used big words as long as I've known him, which is a couple of years, which is a pretty long time. Mom thinks he's odd, but I think he's a genius. It probably helps that his mom is a NASA scientist.

Still, he can be pretty helpless for a genius.

"Here," I say, snatching his glasses and cleaning them with a dry patch on my shorts.

It's a good thing, too, because as soon as Tommy puts them back on, he makes the discovery of the summer. No, the discovery of the year. No, the discovery of the *millennium.*

"Peter, look!"

I scan the canal until I see it—a gray lump floating a few yards away from where we're sitting. It disappears under the water, then pops back up a few seconds later.

"If I had to make a guess," says Tommy, "I'd say that's a—"

"Manatee," I whisper.

A breeze stirs the reeds in the shallows and prickles the back of my neck as I crawl on my hands and knees to the water's edge. The manatee sinks and rises again, and this time its head breaks the water, just for a second—a big, whiskery snout with two nostrils and two beady black eyes.

My heart is flitting like the wings of the ruby-throated hummingbird, a.k.a. Discovery #54. I remind myself to breathe, because sometimes when I get really excited, I hold my breath so long my chest starts to ache and I almost die.

"Journal," I say. Tommy hands it over, and I flip to a fresh page. At the top, I write *Discovery #95: Manatee.* Then I start sketching.

"What're all those white lines on its back?" I say, real quiet so I don't scare it away.

Tommy scoots forward the tiniest bit. "Maybe every

manatee has a unique pattern, the way every giraffe has a unique set of spots. That's just a hypothesis, though."

We sit there for a little while, shoulder to shoulder, me studying the manatee and sketching on the left page of the journal and Tommy jotting down notes and observations and questions on the right. The sun beats down like it's trying to bake us—"There's a twelve percent chance we're about to get heatstroke," Tommy says—but I don't care. Because manatees are real.

I know that sounds silly. Of *course* manatees are real. But until this moment, I wasn't really sure. I couldn't really *know*.

And if manatees are real, maybe Papa's story is real, too.

Papa! I check my watch—Jupiter is twenty-two minutes past three—then stand so fast I almost kick the Discovery Journal into the canal. Tommy yelps, but I dive for the journal and grab it in the nick of time. The manatee disappears under the water in all the commotion.

"I have to go." I don't want to say it—all I want to do is sit here and sketch the manatee for hours—but I can't.

"Already?" Tommy says, standing and brushing grass off his shorts. "I could come over, if you want. I could start my manatee research on your computer. I mean, after I take a shower, and wash off the bacteria—"

"No! I mean, that's okay. We'll talk later. Walkie-talkies."

I hand the journal back to Tommy so he can fill in

Discovery #95 with his research.

"Actually, Peter, there's something I wanted to say. I mean, something I wanted to talk to you about . . ."

"Walkie-talkies!" I say, and then I take off running.

I look back a few times at the canal, but I can't see the manatee. The water is too dirty to see much of anything below the surface. But it'll be here again. It *has* to be here again.

I wince when my feet hit the pavement. It's like dancing across hot coals till I get to my house, the small one on the cul-de-sac between the canal and the highway. I should really start wearing shoes outside.

I head straight for Papa's bedroom, where he always lies down for his afternoon naps.

"Papa, guess what I just saw!"

He's not there.

THREE

"Papa? PAPA?"

The air-conditioning is blasting, but I'm still sweating up a storm as I search the house. I'm pretty sure my heart is beating faster than a ruby-throated hummingbird's right now, and that's saying something, because a hummingbird's heart can beat as fast as 1,200 times a minute, according to Tommy.

Last week, when Mom was coaching me to be Papa's summer caregiver, she said it's important that I give Papa his three o'clock pills right on time. He can get confused if he misses a dose. He also gets confused when he wakes up from a nap, which means right now he might be *super* confused.

He's not in his recliner by the fake fireplace in the living room.

He's not rummaging through the freezer for his chocolate mint ice cream, either.

He's not in the hallway, or Mom's room, or the bathroom, or the laundry room.

I check my room last, and I swear I jump a full foot in the air when I see him there, unscrewing the knob on my closet door with a screwdriver. I guess sometimes even when you're looking for someone, it gives you a good scare when you find them.

But I'm relieved, too. *Really* relieved. This is my first day on Official Caregiver Duty. I can't mess it up already. I can't mess it up at all.

"Papa, what're you doing?"

He stops tinkering with the closet door long enough to look at me. My stomach drops. When Papa is feeling like himself, his eyes are bright and warm and full of all the secrets of the universe. But right now, his eyes are foggy. He doesn't recognize me.

"You're Marianne's friend, aren't you?" he says.

"I'm Peter," I say as calmly as I can. Mom says it's important to stay calm when Papa is confused. Not that *she* always does.

His bushy eyebrows knit together. "Can you get Marianne? It's time to leave the hotel."

"This isn't a hotel, Papa. And Mom—Marianne—it's her first day back at work, remember?"

He looks at the closet door, then down at his red tool-box, which sits open at his feet. Papa used to use his tools to fix things that were broken. Now, more often than not, he uses them to break things that are fine.

"Don't worry," he says, patting my shoulder with a shaky hand. "We can leave as soon as I fix the elevator."

"Papa, that's not—"

I pause and close my eyes and take a deep breath. That's what Mom does when she's trying to calm down: big inhale, big exhale.

But it's pretty hard to be calm right now, because my watch says it's half an hour past three, and Papa thinks my closet is an elevator, and I don't know if I can do this without Mom, and if I can't, she won't be able to go back to work this summer, and she won't be the Space Coast Real Estate Agent of the Year again, and—

I take another deep breath. Maybe it takes more than one.

Then I take Papa's free hand in mine and tug, trying to lead him away from the closet. He won't budge.

"Now, listen," he says, a new edge in his voice that shouldn't be there. "It's time to go home, so you just go get Marianne."

That's when my eyes start to burn. I never cry—I swear

I don't—so it must be my allergies acting up. I don't have allergies year-round like Tommy, but they get bad in the summer sometimes. Or whenever Papa forgets me.

I step into the hallway and lean against the wall and take a few more deep breaths.

I need a plan. Usually, I'm great at coming up with plans. I can make a plan for *anything*. But right now, my brain feels all slow and sticky, like the swamp where Tommy and I found those wood storks (Discovery #17) and Tommy got the toe of his shoe jammed beneath a tree root and I had to tug him loose while he cried and estimated the odds that we would have to sever his foot. (We didn't.)

I pull my phone out of my pocket. My thumb hovers over Mom's number, but I don't want to bother her on her first day back at work. Besides, she's trusting me to handle this. A month ago, when Papa fell and fractured his hip, she quit working to take care of him. But now she's back at work. Now it's my turn.

I put away my phone and run through the caregiver tips that Mom gave me last week. "Don't let Papa do anything dangerous with his tools," I whisper to myself, counting the tips on my fingers as I go. "Remind him to use his walker if his leg gets shaky. Make sure he drinks a glass of water with his pills." But there wasn't anything about how to convince Papa that our house isn't a hotel.

Then I remember what I wanted to tell Papa when I

first got home. I hurry back into my room and say, "Hey, guess what Tommy and I found today?"

Papa looks at me again like he has no idea who I am. I knuckle my eyes—stupid allergies—and say, "A manatee. Down in the canal."

At first, he just stares at me. But then—slowly—his eyes clear and his mouth stretches into a crooked smile. "A manatee?" he says, eyebrows waggling. "I once saw a whole *herd* of manatees. How about that?"

Suddenly breathing is easier. My lungs expand and the world clicks back into place.

He lets me take his hand then, so I lead him to the kitchen for pills and chocolate mint ice cream while he tells me a story I already know by heart.

FOUR

I've always spent summers with Papa. It's just never been like this.

Before he closed up his watch shop, I used to go to work with him on summer days when Mom was busy being a big-time real estate agent. We'd sit on rusty stools at his workbench, and Papa would show me how to replace a watch battery or repair a broken wristband. He showed me how to polish every piece of metal and glass until it shimmered under the shop lights, too.

It wasn't just watches. Papa could fix anything, so people brought him all kinds of broken stuff—clocks, toaster ovens, bicycles—and he got it all working again in no time.

And when he ran out of broken objects to fix, he'd sketch designs for his own inventions—things to make the world a better place, like a water pitcher filter that could turn salt water into fresh drinking water, a.k.a. the Salt-B-Gone Strainer. (Papa let me name that one.) He said his designs were "theoretical," meaning they look cool on paper but might not really work. But I don't know. I always imagined they could.

So I was excited in the winter when Mom told me Papa was moving in with us, even though I knew it was because he had Alzheimer's and couldn't live alone anymore. "Things are going to be different, Peter," Mom said, but I still thought it would be like old times—Papa and me hanging out all day, tinkering and inventing and eating lots and lots of corn chips. We love corn chips.

Some things *are* like old times. Papa still gets dressed every morning in a crisp white T-shirt and blue jeans and sneakers. He still combs his white hair to one side. He still sketches some pretty awesome inventions, too.

But a lot of things *aren't* like old times. Now Papa has to take pills four times a day. Now his left leg shakes so bad that sometimes he can't even walk. And each time he looks at me like I'm a total stranger—like he's forgotten every day and every moment we've ever spent together— my stomach twists into a pretzel-shaped knot.

I know people get old. I know sometimes they get sick or confused. But it's not supposed to happen to Papa. He's supposed to be like . . . like his Tick-Tock Till the End of Time Watch, a solar-powered watch that doesn't need batteries. (He let me name that one, too.) Or the gopher tortoise, a.k.a. Discovery #43, which can live to be almost a hundred years old and makes burrows in the ground that all kinds of different animals use for shelter.

Tommy once asked me if I miss my dad. My parents got divorced when I was seven, and my dad lives in North Carolina now, so I never see him. But I don't really miss him. It's like I told Tommy—why would I bother missing a dad who left when I have a granddad who'd never leave? A granddad who has always been here?

But now sometimes Papa's *not* here, even when we're in the same room. And boy, that really makes my allergies act up.

If I can just take good enough care of him this summer, though, maybe he'll start feeling better. Maybe he'll stop getting so confused. Maybe his brain is like a watch, and it just needs a little help to start working again—and when it does, the world will click back into place for good.

That's why I'm planning on being the best caretaker this world has ever seen.

FIVE

Mom whirls into the house like a hurricane, her high heels click-clacking on the tile floor. "Dad? Peter? Everyone okay?"

She's breathless and sweaty like she ran the whole way home. I'm not sure why she's so worried. She called to check in twenty minutes ago when she was leaving the office, and I told her everything was fine.

"Totally, one hundred percent okay," I say, grinning the way I imagine good caregivers grin after a day of successful caregiving.

I'm sitting on the couch eating an ice pop, one of those really tall, really skinny ones that come in lots of different colors. Papa is in his recliner with the footrest up. After he told me the manatee story—this time one of the manatees swam right underneath Papa's boat and almost lifted it out of the water—he took his pills and ate his ice cream and started sketching designs for his latest invention, a hydro-powered lawnmower.

"Marianne," he says, "have you seen this manatee, too?"

Mom drops her briefcase on the couch. "Manatee? What manatee?"

"There was a manatee in the canal today," I explain. "It's Discovery #95, which means Tommy and I only need five more—"

"Did you take Papa outside?"

"No. I just hung out with Tommy while Papa was napping."

"He shouldn't be walking any more than he has to," she says, click-clacking over to Papa to brush some lint off his shoulder. (She doesn't check *my* shoulder for lint.)

"I still have two legs, you know," Papa says. "They aren't the best legs, but I've still got them."

"You've got to take it easy, Dad. If you fall again, you might actually break that hip."

Papa chuckles. "That's my Marianne. Always worrying." He holds up his sketch for her. "How about this? A lawnmower that harnesses the power of the sea!"

"Just don't hurt yourself trying to build it or I'll have to take away your tools again," Mom says. She's probably thinking back to last week when Papa shocked himself tinkering with an electrical outlet and she hid his toolbox in her bedroom. He found it the next day. I might have helped.

While she takes Papa's empty ice cream bowl into the kitchen, Papa looks at me and sighs the tiniest sigh. I shrug the tiniest shrug. When he's feeling like himself, it's like we have our own secret language. It's the best.

Then I follow Mom into the kitchen with my ice pop.

"So, no problems?" she whispers.

"Nope," I say without missing a beat. Now that Papa is fine, I'm definitely not telling Mom about the closet elevator fiasco, because then I'd have to tell her that I lost track of time hanging out with Tommy and I wasn't here to give Papa his pills right at three o'clock, and that might make me a bad caregiver.

I just have to hope Papa doesn't mention it to her, either. He probably won't. When he's feeling like himself, he doesn't like talking about times when he was confused.

"And you gave him—" Mom says.

"All his pills."

"I have a few house showings tomorrow. Is that okay?"

"We'll be great."

She lets out a long breath. I wonder if she's been holding it all day. "You're the best," she says. "You know that?"

These days, Mom's eyes are always darting everywhere— from Papa to her laptop to her to-do list pinned on the refrigerator. But sometimes, like right now, she pauses and looks me right in the eye. It feels good.

Until she starts to squint at me, which makes me wonder if I have ice pop on my face. "I swear you're looking more like him every day," she says softly.

"Dad?" I say, frowning.

She laughs and tousles my hair. "No. Papa."

I've seen old pictures of Papa—his hair used to be the same sandy color as mine and we have the same deep-set brown eyes. Maybe one day I'll have his bushy eyebrows, too. The thought makes me smile.

"By the way," she says, flipping through a stack of mail on the kitchen counter, "you got something from Carter Middle School." She hands me an envelope. It's addressed to me: *Peter Harrison.* I like that.

Inside is a letter about extracurricular activities at Carter. It includes a list of sports teams and after-school clubs. There are SO MANY. I get a squirmy feeling in my stomach as I scan the list, like I accidentally swallowed a Florida leatherleaf slug, a.k.a. Discovery #87.

The thing is, I *know* my elementary school. I know every nook and cranny of it. I know the teachers and the kids and the playground. And when I try to think about middle school, it's like a big foggy question mark in my brain. I hate big foggy question marks.

But I'm excited, too. Tommy has been going to a private elementary school for supersmart kids while I've been going to public school. But we're *both* going to Carter. We're finally going to be in school together, sitting side by side in class and at the cafeteria and pretty much everywhere else, too.

It's not like Tommy is my *only* friend, but . . . well, he's my only spend-all-summer-together friend. My only watch-nature-documentaries-together-until-midnight friend.

And, if I'm being honest, he's the only friend who never looks at me like I'm weird.

Mom peeks at the letter over my shoulder. "They have a robotics club? I bet Tommy will like that."

She's right, which means I'll be going to robotics club, too. Tommy and I have to do all the same extracurriculars. Obviously.

I pocket the letter, then help Mom cook dinner—spicy fried rice with scrambled egg and hot sauce, the dish Papa and I love almost as much as corn chips.

While we cook, Mom tells me about her day. "These newlyweds, the Robertsons, they've got no sense of their budget. They want to see riverside houses in Merrill Hills. Ha! When they win the lottery, they can call me."

"It could happen," I say. "Mr. Reilly won the lottery."

Mom rolls her eyes as she stirs the rice. "Mr. Reilly lives on a different planet." She pauses and points a rice-covered spoon at me. "Don't repeat that."

I shrug. I mean, who am I going to repeat it to? Besides Tommy. I repeat everything to Tommy.

Then Mom tells me about the Harleys, who have seven dogs and only want to look at houses that have backyard gazebos. She keeps shaking her head, like these people are unbelievable, but she's smiling, too.

I'm pretty sure Mom loves her job. Last year, the local paper named her Space Coast Real Estate Agent of the Year because she sold lots of houses and got really good reviews from her clients. The paper did a whole article about her, and they took her picture, too. A printout of the article is still pinned to the fridge with a seashell magnet, right beneath her to-do list.

While Mom keeps talking—"If they want a gazebo, can't they just build one themselves? I mean, honestly!"—I look at the image of her standing in the front yard of a big house with her arms crossed and a huge smile on her face. She looks very professional.

I don't know if Mom will be Space Coast Real Estate Agent of the Year again, especially since she just took a month off. But if I take awesome care of Papa this summer, Mom can go back to work for a few months, at least, and sell a bunch of houses, and just maybe she'll get her picture in the paper again.

Maybe she'll stop worrying about money, too. She doesn't talk about money in front of me, but I'm pretty great at eavesdropping and I've overheard her on the phone with Dad, saying, "We don't need any financial help, Jon," which means we probably *do* need financial help. Sometimes Mom says the opposite of what she means, especially with Dad.

I don't know why she still talks to him. Whenever he calls me, I just don't pick up. It makes it a whole lot easier to forget he exists.

After dinner, I fetch a sketching pad for Papa because his leg is shaking and he's having a hard time leaving his recliner. "Lawnmower manufacturers won't know what hit 'em," he says. With his back hunched and his head bent over his paper, he almost looks like a kid doing his homework. I don't remember Papa ever looking so small. It makes me feel weird, so I go to my room and grab my walkie-talkie.

"Fox, this is Falcon, over."

A few seconds later, Tommy's voice crackles through the speaker. "Falcon, I'm copying. Over."

Last year Tommy inherited a set of walkie-talkies from his dad, who used them back when he used to go paintballing in the swamp with his work buddies, before he fell out of a tree and broke his arm and Tommy's mom made a no-more-paintballing rule. I've tried to get Tommy to go paintballing in the swamp with me, but he's too chicken, mostly because of his dad's broken arm. Apparently, there's a 37 percent chance of sustaining a moderate to severe injury while paintballing. Who knew?

But the walkie-talkies come in handy. Tommy's house is on the opposite side of the neighborhood, and toy walkie-talkies can't reach that far but these real ones do.

"Did you get a letter from Carter Middle School, too?" I say. "I've already picked out seven extracurriculars for us. Oh, wait—eight. We *have* to do debate club."

"Um," says Tommy. "I don't think I got a letter."

"Weird," I say. "I bet yours is in the mail. Hey, wanna check out the canal? We can see if the manatee is still there."

"I don't know," says Tommy. "There are record numbers of mosquitos out tonight. They said so on the news."

"So?"

"Mosquitos can carry lots of viruses, and I think my immune system is still recovering from all that river bacteria."

I sigh. "How about a nature documentary, then?"

"At your house?" Tommy says.

"At *your* house. Duh. On your big TV."

Silence.

"Fox, do you copy?"

"I—I can't," says Tommy. "But I could ask my parents if I can come over there?"

"No can do. The house is a mess."

It's not exactly true, but it's easier than the truth.

Tommy knows that Papa lives with us, but he doesn't know about Papa's dementia. The last time Tommy was over, I caught Papa walking around in his underwear in the living room. He was lost and looking for his toolbox so he could "fix" the microwave. Tommy was in my room, so he didn't see, but ever since then I've been finding reasons not to invite Tommy over.

But this is the first time Tommy hasn't let me come to *his* house, which seems fishy.

"I've been researching manatees," Tommy says. "I think I found out what those white lines are on its back."

I plop down on my beanbag chair. It's still spilling beans even though Papa put duct tape over the holes. "Are they born with them?"

"The lines are scars. Most manatees have them from getting hit by boats. Some manatees have over fifty scars."

"Fifty?" I didn't count the white lines on the manatee we saw today, but I know there were a lot.

"I found an article from the local paper, too," Tommy says. "There seems to be a fight going on between a local organization called the Florida Manatee Society and the Indigo River Boating Club. The Florida Manatee Society wants boaters to agree to some guidelines they're suggesting, like driving slower in areas where manatees congregate."

"Congregate?"

"Gather," says Tommy.

I peer out my window. It's dark, but I know the canal is out there. Maybe our manatee is, too.

"Why won't the boating club do it?"

"It says that the club's president—"

"Mr. Reilly!" I stand up so fast I get a head rush. "Tommy, meet me at two o'clock sharp tomorrow outside the Reillys' house," I say, because it's a safe bet Papa will nap again after lunch. I'll just have to be quicker getting home this time.

"Uh, Peter . . . are you going to get me in trouble?"

"Have I *ever* gotten you in trouble?"

"Yes," he says. "A lot."

I press my face against the cool glass of the window. I can just make out the dark ribbon of the canal. "Chin up, Fox. It's time to save the world."

"The whole world?"

"Everyone has to start somewhere. You and me, we're starting with a manatee."

SIX

Tommy and I met the summer after third grade, a few weeks after he and his parents moved into the biggest house in the neighborhood, the one with bay windows and blue shutters and a wraparound porch. (I guess NASA scientists and risk analysts can afford nice homes.) I was riding my bike from one end of the neighborhood to the other and spotted him looking out of a second-story window with his binoculars.

"What d'ya see?" I yelled.

I must've spooked him, because he squealed and almost dropped his binoculars, which made me laugh, but only a little.

"Wakulla seaside sparrow," he said.

I remember thinking his dark curly hair looked a bit

like a Wakulla seaside sparrow's nest. I also remember deciding right then and there that he was going to be my friend. I even told him so that day: "We're friends starting now."

It didn't take us long to realize we both loved animals, so later that summer we formed the Discovery Club. We bought a yellow notebook at the convenience store, covered it in animal stickers, and wrote *Peter and Tommy's Discovery Journal* on the front in big bubble letters. On the very first page, we stated the club's mission: *We, Peter Harrison and Tommy Saunders, do hereby pledge to catalog every animal species we can find in these pages until the journal is complete.* Tommy writes the notes because he's a pro at researching stuff. I do the drawings.

The club was my idea, and it was a pretty genius idea, if you ask me. Mom was working a ton that summer, and on the days that I didn't go to Papa's watch shop, I was super bored. All that my friends from school wanted to do was play video games, which can be fun, but I'd rather have an adventure in real life than an adventure on a screen.

Not that Tommy was up for adventure right away. It took a little while for him to warm up to the idea of being outdoors, not just *looking* at the outdoors through his window—"My immune system isn't used to the local allergens," he said—but once he stopped sneezing every two seconds, the whole looking-for-animals thing got a lot easier.

The first entries were simple enough—white-crowned pigeon, eastern gray squirrel, Florida scrub jay, garter snake. All the animals we could spot around the neighborhood and the canal. (Neighbors' pets don't count. You can't *discover* a pet.)

Then we started riding our bikes along the Indigo River. That's where we found the black-bellied whistling duck. The Mediterranean house gecko. The eastern narrow-mouthed toad. Lots of fish, too—the common snook, the spotted sea trout, and the mahogany snapper that nipped Tommy's toe. We even spotted an alligator once, but Tommy ran away before we could get a good look at it. Okay, we *both* ran away, but Tommy was way more scared than I was.

It's harder to work on the journal during the school year, especially since we haven't been going to the same school. But sometimes on the weekends Tommy's parents will drive us to a state park so we can find rarer animals, like beavers and armadillos and snowy egrets.

Tommy and I promised each other we'd finish the journal before we start middle school together this fall. It's tricky because we're running out of animals, but that just makes it more exciting when we do find one.

And the manatee? That's the best one yet. I've been

waiting to find a manatee ever since Papa first told me his story, and now that I've found one, I'm going to make sure nobody adds another scar to its back. And that includes Mr. Reilly.

SEVEN

Tommy winces as I give the Reillys' door three good raps with my knuckles.

"There's a very high probability that this is a bad idea," he says, voice quivering. "I don't know the exact percentage, but . . . *very high.*"

"Oh, stop. This is the best idea I've had in months," I say. "Well, maybe in weeks. I have lots of good ideas."

Mrs. Reilly answers the door in a fuzzy robe with her hair up in curlers. An icy blast of air-conditioned air washes over my sweaty face.

"Well, hi, boys! You having a nice summer?"

"Yes, ma'am," Tommy and I say.

I won't call Mr. Reilly *sir*, but I'm okay calling Mrs. Reilly *ma'am* because she's not a bully like him. She spends most of her time tanning in their front yard on a lawn chair, holding a car sunshade in front of her face, and I'm pretty sure that doesn't hurt any manatees, though it's probably not so great for her skin. Plus, she doesn't seem to like Mr. Reilly very much, even though they're married. (I really don't understand marriage.)

"It's hard, the way things change," she says, giving us a sad smile. "But that's life sometimes, isn't it?"

"Yes, ma'am," we say again, even though I have no idea what she's talking about. Tommy wriggles and inches toward the bushes by the door.

Mrs. Reilly nods. "I'm about to make some changes myself, truth be told. Sometimes you just have to take the plunge. You can't let life pass you by, can you?"

"Um," I say, "is Mr. Reilly home?"

"Eddie!" Mrs. Reilly hollers over her shoulder. "Get over here!"

While I wait for my archnemesis, Mrs. Reilly leans against the doorframe, still sad-smiling down at us. It's so bright outside that my eyes can't make much sense of the room behind her, but I see a ginormous flat-screen TV and an air hockey table. The Reillys' house isn't very fancy on the outside—it's painted a gross mustard color and the yard is a mess, full of rotting avocados—but the inside looks pretty epic. Winning the lottery must be nice.

When Mr. Reilly finally stalks out of the darkness,

Tommy moves a little closer to the bushes, but I stand my ground.

"Well, well, look who it is," Mr. Reilly says. He's wearing a button-up shirt covered in tropical flowers, but he must have buttoned it wrong, because the left side is hanging down lower than the right.

Mrs. Reilly pokes him in the ribs—"Be *nice*, Eddie, Lord save you"—and slips back into the house, her curlers bobbing as she walks.

I stand as tall as I can—I'm on a growth spurt, so I'm getting taller by the day—and clear my throat because I mean business. "Mr. Reilly, did you know that some manatees have more than forty scars—"

"Fifty," Tommy whispers from the bushes.

"Did you know that some manatees have more than *fifty* scars from being hit by boats?"

Mr. Reilly scratches his face. The sound of his fingernails on his stubbly cheeks makes me cringe. "And?" he says.

"Since you're the president of the Indigo River Boating Club, we"—I glance at Tommy, who is now pretending to be a bush—"*we* believe it's your responsibility to help protect the manatees."

I give Tommy my you're-a-part-of-this-too look—it's a very fierce look—until he starts talking.

"Y-You see, sir," he says, "if the Indigo River Boating

Club adopted certain measures, like going slower in designated manatee zones, then . . . then . . ." His voice peters out like a dying speedboat engine.

Mr. Reilly snorts. "If manatees don't want to get hit, maybe they should get out of the way. If you see a boat coming, do you swim right into it?"

"What are you talking about?" I say. "They're not *trying* to swim into boats!"

"There's a hierarchy here, boys," Mr. Reilly says knowingly. He holds one hand up by his head. "Humans are up here, see?" He places his other hand by his waist. "Animals are down here. We're in charge. It's the way of the world, the . . . whaddya call it? The circle of life."

"That's definitely *not* what the circle of life means. Just because animals aren't human doesn't mean they're not important. If we're more powerful than they are, that just means we can help protect them!"

Mr. Reilly tries to laugh, but it turns into a cough. "I remember what it's like being a kid," he says, tapping his head. "Big, squishy brain full of big, squishy ideas. But when you grow up, you're going to see the world's a mean place. It's every man and manatee for himself. Do you think I'd be where I am today if I wasted time looking out for every stupid thing that breathes? That's not how you get to be president of the Indigo River Boating Club, kid." He jabs a thumb over his shoulder. "It's not how you afford that top-of-the-line air hockey table, either. You've gotta work hard, play hard."

"But *do* you work hard?" I ask. "Or did you just win the lottery?"

Mr. Reilly's mouth curls into a snarl. "Now, listen here. This is my property, and I've already told the two of you to stay off it, so I suggest you leave before I—"

Mrs. Reilly's voice rings out from inside the house. "Eddie, are you being nice?"

"Yes, Elaine," he croaks over his shoulder. Then he cranes his long neck forward so his sun-crisped face is almost touching mine. I can hear his jaw clicking as he gnaws on his invisible tobacco.

"Before I report you both to the . . . the . . . homeowners' association," he says. He turns on Tommy. "Or how about I have a little chat with your parents? They might have to throw in more than a new porch screening when they hear about this."

"But you aren't *listening*!" I yell. I don't mean to yell—I never mean to yell—but when I get this blood-boiling, about-to-breathe-fire feeling, I can't help it. "Have you ever looked at a manatee's back? Have you *seen* the scars? If the Indigo River Boating Club would just work with the Florida Manatee Society—"

The door slams shut in my face.

I raise my fists, ready to pound that door down, but

Tommy puts his hand on my arm. "Peter, there's a one hundred percent chance that knocking again is a bad idea."

"Oh, what do you know?" I say, shrugging him off and stomping away from the house. "You're just scared."

I try taking deep breaths but I can't get enough air. It must be the humidity. The air's so thick it's like I'm walking through stew. Mosquito-and-stinky-fish stew, which is definitely the worst kind of stew.

"Sorry," I say when I get that pinprick of guilt in my chest, the one I feel whenever I snap at Tommy. "I just hate him so much. How can somebody be that heartless? And why does he have to treat us like we're just stupid kids?"

"Well, we're not stupid," Tommy says, ducking his head to avoid a green darner dragonfly, a.k.a. Discovery #39. "But according to society, we *are* kids."

"Soon we'll be in middle school and then people won't be able to treat us like that anymore. Right?"

I wait for him to say yes. I wait for him to say that there's a 110 percent chance we'll be taken seriously once we're in sixth grade. But he doesn't say anything. He just fiddles with the settings on his binoculars. His eyes have that faraway look in them, which means he's probably thinking about osmosis, or black holes, or chlorophyll.

I poke him in the arm. "Fox, do you copy?"

I'm surprised he doesn't jump. Tommy's usually pretty easy to startle. "Copy, Falcon," he says quietly.

"Hey," I say, "why does Mr. Reilly keep asking about your porch screening?"

Tommy opens his mouth, but instead of saying anything, he just shrugs. I give him a suspicious look. Sometimes I wish I could read his mind, but I don't know. It would be a LOT of risk estimates and science facts.

We walk along the canal—me down by the water, Tommy a few feet farther up the grassy slope—until we reach the spot where we saw the manatee yesterday. Today, there are no gray lumps in sight.

"Do you think it swam away?" I say.

"Maybe," says Tommy. "But according to my research, manatees can stay underwater for up to twenty minutes at a time before coming up for air."

I check my solar system watch. The little planet Earth on the hour hand is getting pretty close to three o'clock. "Well, I hope it hurries up. What else did you find out?"

Tommy flips open the Discovery Journal to the manatee entry. The whole right page is covered in his teeny-tiny handwriting.

"'Manatees, also known as sea cows, are marine herbivores that are distantly related to elephants,'" he recites. "'There are three species of manatee, including the West Indian manatee, which can be found in the shallow coastal waters of Florida.'"

While he talks, something beneath the water catches

my eye—something big, drifting toward the bank. Toward us. I crouch between the reeds, trying to see into the water, but it's hard because of the sun's glare. I lose sight of the shape, then wonder if I just imagined it.

"'Some grow as big as thirteen feet long and weigh up to one thousand three hundred pounds,'" Tommy goes on. "'They can live up to sixty years, and they have exceptionally good long-term memory.'"

Wait—there it is again! It's not just big, it's *massive*, and it's moving closer toward us, and closer, until . . .

"'On an average day,'" Tommy says, "'a manatee spends most of its time sleeping or grazing on underwater plants. When they graze, they use their fins to walk along the sandy bottom of riverbeds.'"

Suddenly a manatee breaks the surface right in front of me, its back emerging like a gray rubbery island speckled with algae. I'm a little afraid, which is weird. I'm almost never afraid of animals. But this one is *so big.*

"'Manatees are known for being very gentle,'" Tommy concludes.

I relax and scooch closer to the water.

"Whoa!" says Tommy, finally looking up from the journal. "How long has she been there?"

"She swam over when you started reading. Hey, how do you know she's a *she*?"

"An educated guess," says Tommy. "Female manatees

are usually bigger than males, and this one's pretty big."

"No kidding!"

Part of me wants to touch the manatee, but one of the rules of the Discovery Club is "Respect All Wildlife," and that means looking, not touching. So I look. My eyes trace the white scars on her back, running every which way like a million little roads on a big gray map.

"She's definitely the same one as yesterday. I remember that scar pattern. It looks like a Z, doesn't it?"

Tommy adjusts his glasses and squints. "Sort of," he says.

"You have to get *closer.*"

Tommy takes the tiniest step forward. I roll my eyes.

Then the manatee raises its snout above the water and snorts out a jet of stinky air right in my face. I burst out laughing because I just can't help it. Looking into its beady eyes, I don't feel so mad at Mr. Reilly, or so worried about Papa, or so annoyed at Tommy's fear of rip currents. I feel light, like a green darner dragonfly. Like I could float away on the heavy air. I wonder if this is how Papa felt when he met the manatees.

"She's beautiful," I say. "A beautiful gray blob." I try to waggle my eyebrows the way Papa does when he tells his story, but I think I just end up making a weird face and scaring the manatee, because she dips her snout back under the water.

She doesn't swim away, though. She keeps hovering in the shallows beside us, and a few minutes later, she comes up for more air.

We stay like that for a little while, me and Tommy and the manatee, and I'm pretty sure I could sit here all afternoon.

But I know my time is almost up. Papa is bound to wake from his nap any second now, and he'll need his pills.

I grab the journal so I can work on my manatee sketch for just a minute before I go.

"Zoe," I say.

"Hmm?" says Tommy.

I point to the Z-shaped scar on her back. "Her name is Zoe."

"She probably doesn't have a name. She might have certain vocalizations that allow other manatees to identify her, though."

But I've already written *Zoe* in the journal.

EIGHT

For the rest of the first week of summer vacation, Tommy and I see Zoe in the canal every day. We keep visiting her even after we finish the manatee entry in the Discovery Journal. It's not that she does anything super exciting. She mostly just floats, and sinks, and rises, and munches on algae. But whenever I sit on the bank and watch her, it's like time pauses, and my brain goes all quiet and still—which is pretty wild, because my brain is *never* quiet or still.

Plus, Papa likes hearing my daily Zoe reports.

It's weird, but whenever Papa gets confused, talking about Zoe seems to help. He says he wants to go down to the canal and meet her. I want him to meet her, too, but Mom would lose it if I took Papa outside. "He's one more fall away from breaking his hip," she says. So for now, I'm his eyes and ears. Being the world's greatest caretaker means keeping him safe.

And I'm *totally* on my way to being the world's greatest caretaker. I give Papa his pills and lunches every day this week that Mom goes to work. On Wednesday, he gets pretty confused again—he tries to call Nana to tell her he's working late at the shop, even though Nana's been gone for years and the watch shop is a laundromat now—but I bring up Zoe and get him to tell me his manatee story again. Works like a charm.

Then, on Thursday, Tommy and I find a grasshopper sparrow, bringing us up to ninety-six entries and a couple of pages closer to finishing the journal.

So by Friday, after a week of mostly successful caregiving and two new discoveries, I'm feeling like a champion.

Until Mom gets home from work.

I'm sitting at the kitchen table with a sketchbook while Papa uses his tools to take apart the lamp beside his recliner. (I made sure it was unplugged.) Besides the Discovery Journal, I have a bunch of sketchbooks where I draw all kinds of animals. Today, I'm practicing my manatees.

That's when Mom storms into the house with that pinched look on her face that means someone—probably me—is about to get in trouble.

"Peter, what did I tell you about leaving Mr. Reilly alone?"

"Um . . . You told me not to steal his avocados again?"

"I told you not to *bother* him again. I just ran into him outside, and he says you and Tommy came knocking at his door a few days ago, accusing him of killing manatees. What's all this about?"

Good grief. Mr. Reilly can really exaggerate things. "We didn't say he was *killing* anything, we just said—"

"Mr. Reilly isn't a good person to upset, Peter."

I actually think Mr. Reilly is a *great* person to upset, but before I can say so, Mom drops her voice and says, "And how long did you leave Papa alone while you were stirring up trouble with the neighbors?"

Oh boy. I can feel my face getting red. Because I *didn't* go to Mr. Reilly's to stir up trouble. I went to defend manatees. And except for Monday when I got home a little late and Papa thought my closet was an elevator, I've been a real pro at caregiving.

"You said I could hang out with Tommy while Papa is napping!" I whisper-yell, trying really hard not to *actually* yell.

Mom squeezes her eyes shut. I can tell by the way her nostrils flare that she's practicing her deep breathing. She practices her deep breathing a lot, especially around me.

She opens her eyes. "You're right. I'm sorry. But maybe you could have Tommy over here when you want to hang out, at least while I'm at work."

"But we can't find any animals in the house, except for some lizards, and Tommy thinks we've already covered all the lizards native to central Florida!"

"I know, Peter. But some things are more important than—"

"Plus, I don't *want* to have Tommy over here!" I'm actually yelling now. I know I should probably stop because I've got that chest-on-fire feeling and that means I'm about to say something I'll regret, but I just keep going. "It's *embarrassing*. Papa might say something weird, or . . . or . . . walk around in his underwear again!"

I clamp my hands over my mouth, but I know it's too late. Mom goes back to her deep breathing, which makes me feel bad enough, but then I see Papa. He's turned around in his recliner with the lamp base in one hand and a screwdriver in the other, looking right at me. That fiery feeling in my chest turns into white-hot shame.

These days, Papa's eyes can go from bright to dim and back again, all in the course of a day. They're like those variable stars Tommy told me about. They can't decide how much they want to shine. But right now, beneath his bushy eyebrows, his eyes are as clear as the summer sky.

"I know this isn't easy," Mom begins. I don't let her finish. I leave my sketchbook and drawing pencils on the kitchen table and run to my room. I don't come out all night, not even for dinner. When Mom brings me a plate, I tell her I'm not hungry. I tell her that I don't feel well.

Which is true. I might not have a fever or a broken arm, but my brain definitely doesn't feel good. This week had been going so well, and now I've messed it all up. Good caregivers don't say the sort of thing that I just said. Good caregivers don't hurt the people they're caring for. They don't get embarrassed by them, either.

I'm NOT embarrassed by Papa, I tell myself.

But what if I am?

I used to be so proud of Papa. I used to tell everyone all about him and his inventions. On Bring Your Parent to School Day, when everyone brought their moms or dads, I brought Papa. He was a big hit.

So being embarrassed by him now . . . well, it feels like betraying him. And Papa is the last person in the world I want to betray.

I just want to sleep, but later that night, when Mom and Papa have gone to bed and the house is perfectly quiet, I realize I *can't* sleep. I toss and turn until my sheets feel warm and itchy; then I shake them off and grab my walkie-talkie.

"Fox, this is Falcon. Do you copy?"

A full minute passes before Tommy's voice crackles through the speaker. "Falcon, I think you just interrupted me in the middle of a REM cycle."

I roll my eyes, but boy, I don't know what I'd do without Tommy.

NINE

Mom has an early morning house showing on Saturday, so I sit on the couch in my pajamas and drink orange juice and watch a gorilla documentary on TV while Papa reads the newspaper in his recliner. I think we're the only house in the neighborhood that still gets a physical copy of *Space Coast Today* delivered each morning. Papa has always loved reading the newspaper, so Mom subscribed when he moved in with us.

"Says here there have been a lot of shark sightings lately," he says. "How about that?"

Papa knows I love animals more than anything. But I don't know what to say to him, not after yesterday. And not if he's going to be this nice. Why isn't he mad at me? Why isn't he telling me I'm the worst caregiver in the world, not to mention the worst grandson? I want to apologize again, but I think the words are stuck in my throat. Maybe the orange juice will dislodge them. I take another gulp. No luck.

When Mom gets home, she makes waffles and the three of us sit around the kitchen table and eat the most awkward breakfast ever. Mom stares at me. She doesn't look angry. She just looks worried. And that makes everything worse, because she should be mad at me, too. *Somebody* should be mad at me, or else I'll just have to be mad at myself!

Mom's phone rings before we finish eating. It must be a client because she starts pacing the living room and talking about down payments and mortgages.

I set down my fork. I'm not hungry. I feel too heavy and sad and mad and I-don't-know-what-else. I need to go outside. I need to see Zoe.

"If Mom asks," I say, "can you let her know I'm by the canal?"

I want Papa to tell me I can't go outside, not unless I ask Mom first. I want him to tell me I'm a bad grandson *and* a bad son. But he doesn't. He just gives me a nod and a wink. So while Mom explains property taxes to her client, I slip out of the house and down to the water.

There's a buzzing feeling in the air, the one that means a thunderstorm is coming, and the sky is thick with clouds. As I kneel by the canal and splash water on my arms and legs, I hear thunder rumbling in the distance.

I scan the water for Zoe. It takes me a few minutes—it's hard to find a gray lump when the whole world is gray—but finally I spot her floating near the Reillys' dock.

"Zoe!" I call, trying to make my voice louder than the thunder. But she doesn't move.

Actually . . . she's not moving at all. She's not sinking, or rising, or munching on algae. I don't even think she's floating. It looks like she's beached in the shallows.

The first fat raindrops hit my skin as I race around the end of the canal. I stumble down the bank to where she's lying, and that's when I see the cut on her back—a fresh one, pink and red and awful. A wave of nausea rocks me. I can only look at the cut for a second before I have to close my eyes.

The rain is picking up, turning into a roar and needling my skin. I open my eyes and see that Zoe's are open, too—open and looking back at me. She's alive, but I know she's hurting. Really hurting.

My mind races. Zoe is beached by Mr. Reilly's dock. Which means she was probably hit by a boat here. Which means Mr. Reilly was probably the one who did it.

I want to run up and bang on the Reillys' door until it splinters into a million pieces. I don't care if Mr. Reilly isn't a "good person to upset." I want to tell him exactly what I think of him. I want to report *him* to the homeowners' association, or better yet, the police—

No. First things first. Zoe needs help and I need a plan. Maybe there's a way to treat her cut. Maybe I could clean it. Maybe I could bandage it. I need . . . towels, I think. And waterproof bandages. And . . . I don't know *what* all I need, but I'm not going to find it here by the canal.

"Wait here," I tell Zoe. "I'll be right back. I promise!"

The sky crackles as I sprint up the bank and down the road. I don't know where I'm going until I find myself standing on the doorstep of Tommy's house, panting and soaked to the bone. I knock on his front door as hard as I can and don't stop until his dad opens it.

"What on earth—oh, hey there, Peter! Is everything okay? Here, get out of the rain."

"Everything is *not* okay. There's an injured manatee in the canal and—"

I freeze when I look past Mr. Saunders and see that Tommy's living room is full of cardboard boxes. "What's going on? What are all those boxes for?"

"The big move!" says Mr. Saunders, opening his arms wide like I don't know what *big* means.

"What big move?"

"The move to Michigan? Next month?"

Rain streaks from my hair down into my eyes and makes everything blurry.

"Michigan?"

"Surely Tommy told you?"

I stare at him. He's playing a trick on me. I know he is. Tommy can't be moving to Michigan. I mean, who moves to Michigan?

But then I see Tommy, and I know by the look on his face that this is no trick.

TEN

Tommy and I stare at each other. Rain beats the house like a drum and rattles through the gutters. There are a million things I think of saying—a million questions I think of asking—but I can't speak. I guess Tommy can't, either. His mouth gapes but nothing comes out. All I can do is read his face—a flicker reel of shame and sadness.

I wonder what he sees in my face. Can he see the confusion? The shock? What about the anger, swelling like a tidal wave? There are too many feelings. They rattle inside me like the rain in the gutters until I can't tell what any of them are saying.

I shut my eyes tight and scrunch up my face and take deep breaths, one after the other, so I don't explode into a million pieces. Then I remind myself why I came here. I remember my promise to Zoe. Everything else has to wait.

"Zoe's hurt," I say, finding my voice somewhere deep inside me. "Mr. Reilly hit her with his boat, so we need to—"

"Mr. Reilly hit someone?" Mr. Saunders says, eyes bugging. With his thick glasses and black, curly hair, he looks a lot like future Tommy.

"Zoe is a manatee," I say.

"Ah. Was this one of your discoveries?"

Mr. Saunders frowns when he says *discoveries*. Maybe he's remembering Discovery #61, which was a raccoon that Tommy and I found in Tommy's backyard and accidentally let inside. It ran into Mr. Saunders's home office and peed on his keyboard and ate his almonds. But good grief, he should really be over that by now.

"She's in the canal by Mr. Reilly's dock," I say. "I need towels, and bandages, and whatever you use to clean a cut to make sure it's not infected. But it has to be safe for manatees."

"Hold on," says Mr. Saunders. "Let's think about this for a moment. I'm sure there's someone we can call to report the injury."

"The Florida Manatee Society," Tommy says quietly. "That's the organization I was telling you about, Peter. I bet they'll know what to do."

I'm about to tell Tommy that we don't have time to call

anyone because Zoe needs help *now*. That I can help her—I can fix this—if I just get the right supplies.

But . . . I'm not 100 percent sure how to bandage a manatee. I'm not even 50 percent sure, actually. And I definitely don't want to hurt her by trying to help her. Maybe the Florida Manatee Society can tell me what to do.

"Okay," I say, "but we have to *hurry!*"

"We can check their website for a phone number," Tommy says.

"Maybe I should make the call?" Mr. Saunders says, but I'm already racing to Tommy's room, weaving through an obstacle course of cardboard boxes and passing Mrs. Saunders in the hall.

"Peter!" she says. "It's nice to see you."

"Injured manatee! Talk later!"

There are boxes in Tommy's room, too—open boxes overflowing with Tommy's things, like his *Birds of the American Southeast* book that we've spent hours reading together, and the microscope that we used to study leaves for my fifth-grade science fair project last spring. His walls, which used to be covered in NASA posters, are bare now. I feel dizzy, like the world is turning inside out. Like a wave just dragged me under and I can't tell which way is up.

But I'm not going to think about Tommy or boxes or Michigan right now. I'm thinking about Zoe and only Zoe.

One thing at a time. While Tommy looks up the Florida Manatee Society website on his computer, I practice my deep breathing—in through the nose and out through the mouth, just the way Mom taught me.

"Here," he says, clicking on a *Contact Us* link.

I look over his shoulder at the screen and dial the society's number into my phone. It rings once, twice, three times . . . Ugh! What's the point of having a phone number if you aren't going to answer?!

I'm about to hang up, but then: "Thanks for calling the Florida Manatee Society, central Florida's largest-running—I mean, *longest*-running—manatee research and advocacy center! My name is Cassidy Cawley and I'm—"

"I need to know how to help an injured manatee," I say. "Her name is Zoe—well, that's what I call her—and she's cut up bad. She's in the canal in my neighborhood, which is in a town called Stonecrest, which is next to the highway, and if you want to know who's to blame, it's probably this guy Mr. Reilly. He lives in an ugly yellow house and he should definitely go to jail."

When I pause for breath, Cassidy says, "Oh god. Okay, an injured manatee. So, I need to call the Florida Marine Life Commission—"

"We don't have time!" I yell. "Can't you just tell me what to do?"

"Wait—don't do anything!" she says, which is just about

the worst sentence I've ever heard in my entire life. "I mean, you did the right thing by reporting the injury, but please don't touch the manatee. The Marine Life Commission will send people out. And . . . maybe I should come, too? I mean, usually Maria Liu would come—she's my boss—but she's out of town today, so . . . I guess it's me?"

"How should I know?!"

"Sorry! It's actually my first day working here. I mean, I used to be an intern, but . . ." Cassidy exhales long and slow. I guess she takes deep breaths when she's stressed, too. "I'll be right there. I mean, not *right there*, but soon. Our office is a few towns away. I think." *Click.*

I turn and see Mr. and Mrs. Saunders standing in the doorway to Tommy's room, staring at me like I'm a raccoon who just peed on a keyboard.

"Everything okay, boys?" says Mrs. Saunders slowly.

"Why don't you show us this manatee?" says Mr. Saunders.

Before I can decide whether or not I want the help of people who are moving to Michigan and completely deserting me and basically ruining my life, my phone rings.

"Right, so, I need an address," says Cassidy.

ELEVEN

Twenty minutes later, it's still pouring rain and nobody has showed up to help.

I'm sitting by the canal with an umbrella that Mrs. Saunders lent me, holding it so it covers a little bit of me and a little bit of Zoe. Behind me, Tommy and his parents are huddled beneath an avocado tree near Mr. Reilly's dock.

I told them they could go home. But a few minutes ago, when Mom ran down to the canal looking for me, Mr. and Mrs. Saunders explained the situation and promised her they'd keep an eye on me while we waited for the Florida Marine Life Commission to arrive.

I overheard them talking about the move to Michigan, too. "We thought you both knew," Mrs. Saunders said. "We thought Tommy had already told Peter."

But I tuned all of that out, because I'm still focusing on Zoe and only Zoe. When Mom tried to get me to go home—"It's a *monsoon* out here, Peter"—I told her I'm not leaving for anything. So she ran home to be with Papa, and I stayed right here, right next to Zoe.

She's still alive—her beady eyes are looking back into mine—but I don't know how much time she has left. And I hate that I can't do anything except sit here and wait for someone else to fix this. I hate it so much it hurts.

I look at the road, then at my watch. Twenty-two minutes now, but it feels like twenty-two hours. What's taking so long? Doesn't anybody care about Zoe?

Finally, a tiny green car putters into our neighborhood. It rumbles down the road in fits and starts, engine wheezing, then lurches to a stop by the end of the canal. A woman wearing a rain jacket and jean shorts and bright purple sneakers hops out.

"Peter?" she calls. I recognize the voice of Cassidy Cawley.

"Over here!"

Her sneakers squelch in the mud as she slip-slides toward us, cutting through the Reillys' backyard. I'm surprised Mr. Reilly isn't out here yelling at us to get off his property. He's probably too busy playing air hockey, or watching something stupid on his giant TV, or— I push away thoughts of my archnemesis. One thing at a time.

"Oh no," Cassidy says, kneeling next to me in the grass and holding her hand above Zoe's nostrils. "Okay, so, the good news is she's breathing."

"And the bad news?" Mrs. Saunders says. She joins us down by the bank along with Tommy and Mr. Saunders. Tommy's glasses are streaked with rain. I can't see his eyes.

Cassidy brushes a clump of wet hair off her forehead. "I think this is one of the deepest cuts I've ever seen on a manatee."

I take a closer look at Cassidy. She has freckly cheeks, a small nose, and an overbite. She looks young—well, young for an adult. "Isn't this your first day?"

"It's my first day of *this* job," she says. "But I've interned with the Florida Manatee Society before, and I have a degree in marine biology, and I studied manatees in college?" I don't know why she turns it into a question. I also don't know what the answer is.

"The MLC—that's the Marine Life Commission—they should be here any minute," she says. Then, under her breath: "God, I wish Maria was here."

Mr. and Mrs. Saunders retreat back under the avocado tree. I expect Cassidy to follow them, but she doesn't. She stays right next to me and Zoe.

So does Tommy. I'm pretty sure this is the closest he's gotten to the canal since the rip current. If I wasn't so furious with him, I might be proud of him.

"I'm sorry, Peter," he whispers, so soft I almost can't hear him over the hiss of the rain. "I meant to tell you. I *tried* to tell you."

I don't say anything. I don't look at him. I just keep watching Zoe.

A couple minutes later, a Florida Marine Life Commission van and a few cars pull into the neighborhood. Most of the people who get out of the van and the cars are wearing MLC T-shirts, which feels official and good but also kind of scary. Maybe calling the Florida Manatee Society was a mistake. Maybe I should've figured out how to help Zoe myself.

"What are they going to do to her? They're not going to hurt her, are they?"

"They're going to help her," says Cassidy. "Well . . . they're going to try."

Try. I hate that word.

Cassidy waves everyone over, and then there are too many people and too many things going on, and the world is getting loud and fuzzy, like radio static turned up to max volume. A woman in an MLC shirt asks me and Tommy to step aside, and then everyone crowds around the canal until I can't see Zoe anymore. They're all talking at once and the rain is still pouring and I can't hear what anyone is saying, and nobody thinks to tell me what's going on, even though I'm the one who called about Zoe and I'm the one who knows her and I'm the one whose heart will break if she doesn't make it.

Then another van is driving into the neighborhood—a Channel 9 local news van—and a camerawoman and a guy with a poncho and a microphone are joining the crowd. Some neighbors are coming out of their houses to see what all the fuss is about, too. I see Mrs. Reilly talking to Tommy's parents, but no sign of Mr. Reilly. Surprise, surprise. Of course he'd flee the scene of the crime.

I look everywhere at once, trying to find a way I can help. But it's too noisy. It's too busy. I don't know what's going on. The only thing I know is that someone is backing up the MLC van toward the canal, and the tires are squealing in the wet grass, and mud is flying everywhere. Then people are dragging a ginormous fishing net out of the van and lowering it into the water around Zoe.

"What're you doing to her?" I yell. "What's happening?"

"I think they're taking her out of the water," says Tommy, his hand on my arm.

I shake him off. "No—just—wait a second! Stop!"

I don't know if I'm telling Tommy to stop talking or if I'm telling everyone else to get away from Zoe or if I'm telling my allergies to knock it off because my eyes are on fire right now. I just need *everything* to stop. I need to put the world on pause. Why doesn't the world have a pause button?

Now all the adults—including Cassidy and Tommy's parents and Mrs. Reilly—are grabbing hold of the net and heaving Zoe out of the water. I can't watch. I can't *not* watch. Everyone is grunting and cursing. "Heaven help us, she's heavy!" Mrs. Reilly cries.

I try to join them, but I can't find an open spot. It's a wall of backs and elbows. "Be careful!" I scream. "Don't hurt her!"

Finally, they drag Zoe onto a big blue tarp that someone laid in the grass. I expect her to thrash around or try to get back to the water, but when I catch a glimpse of her through all the bodies, she's perfectly still, which is even worse.

While MLC workers clean her wound and give her shots, I keep fighting to get to her side, but I can't. I'm stuck on the outskirts like I'm a stranger. Like I don't know her at all.

Behind me, the reporter in the poncho is talking fast into the camera. "This manatee was discovered with a nasty cut, and as you can see here, a heroic group of Marine Life Commission workers and volunteers are helping her into the van, which will take her to the manatee rehabilitation center at Emerald Springs State Park . . ."

Now everyone is gathering around the tarp, lifting it,

hauling Zoe into the back of the van. The camerawoman cuts in front of me, blocking my view. "Move!" I bellow, but the doors of the van slam shut before I can get another look at Zoe.

I'm still straining to get a clear view of the van when Tommy's parents find us. They're drenched and muddy, breathing hard.

"Man, oh man!" says Mr. Saunders. "That was a workout!"

"Are you boys okay?" says Mrs. Saunders.

Tommy nods, but I don't bother answering because it's a stupid question. Of course I'm not okay. I barrel through the crowd milling around the van until I find Cassidy.

"She's going to make it, isn't she?" I say. "She *has* to make it."

"I hope so," Cassidy says. "Most manatees survive these kinds of cuts, but I can't say for sure yet. Whatever happens, you did the right thing by reporting the injury!"

"But how do you *know* it's the right thing? What if Zoe doesn't survive the drive? What if all those shots you guys gave her actually hurt her? What if I didn't spot the cut soon enough? What if—"

"The MLC will do everything they can," she says. "I'm sure they will. And Emerald Springs State Park—that's a good place for her. I know a guy who works there. I mean, a friend. I mean, he *is* a guy, but just a friend. A friend-guy."

Cassidy's freckly cheeks turn crimson red. "Anyway, he'll take good care of her."

"EDDIE!"

Cassidy and I whip around and find Mrs. Reilly standing beside us, waving in the direction of her patio. I follow her gaze until I see him, too—Mr. Reilly, sitting there totally sheltered from the storm, staring at us like we're all part of a boring TV show and he doesn't know how to change the channel.

"We could've used an extra pair of hands out here, you know!" Mrs. Reilly hollers.

Mr. Reilly shrugs. That's it—no words, just a shrug. His words echo through my head: *It's every man and manatee for himself. Do you think I'd be where I am today if I wasted time looking out for every stupid thing that breathes?*

Suddenly I feel madder than I've ever felt in my entire life. I feel like a bolt of lightning ready to strike down on Mr. Reilly's porch and set his world on fire. I barely even notice the camera pointed at me until the poncho man says, "Are you the boy who found the manatee?"

I face the camera and blink rainwater out of my eyes. Behind the camerawoman, Tommy and Mr. and Mrs. Saunders and Cassidy are all watching me.

"I am," I say. "Her name is Zoe, and I know exactly who's to blame for hurting her."

Then I point at Mr. Reilly. The camera follows my finger until it's pointed at him, too.

"Well, now, that's quite the claim!" the reporter says. "And how do you—"

"And that's enough for this interview!" Mrs. Saunders says, steering me away from the camera and the reporter and the Reillys and everyone and everything.

TWELVE

I am the star of the nightly news.

There must not be a lot happening in central Florida today, because Channel 9 plays the footage of Zoe getting pulled out of the canal over and over again. They play my interview over and over again, too.

"This kid isn't afraid to name names," the news anchor says. "Or point fingers, at least!"

And there I am again. *"Her name is Zoe, and I know exactly who's to blame for hurting her."*

The camera swings toward the Reillys' patio, and if you squint at the TV screen, you can just barely see Mr. Reilly's jaw shifting from side to side as he chews his invisible tobacco.

After the clip, the anchor chuckles. "Let's see that one more time."

Mom does not chuckle. Mom is furious. "What on *earth* possessed you to say such a thing to someone with a *camera*?"

I look at Papa and sigh the tiniest sigh. He shrugs the tiniest shrug. And it feels good, like maybe Papa and I are okay, even though I was such a jerk yesterday about not having Tommy over. It might be the only thing about today that feels good.

"I had to say *something*," I say. "If nobody stops Mr. Reilly and the Indigo River Boating Club, they'll just hurt more manatees!"

"Saving manatees isn't your job, Peter."

"It *is* my job. It's everyone's job."

"You know what I mean," she says, even though I don't. "And you have no way of knowing Mr. Reilly injured her."

"Why are you defending him? You know what he's like!"

"I'm not *defending* him—"

We're interrupted by a banging on the front door. Mom huffs. "We'll continue this conversation later."

She storms over to the door and throws it open. Just my luck—it's Mr. Reilly. I hide out of sight in the hallway and listen as he complains to Mom about how I tried to "assassinate his character on live TV."

"Look, I'm sure he didn't mean it," Mom says. "We just found out today about the Saunderses moving, and I think Peter's taking the news hard. Tommy is his best—"

"You know, there are other real estate agents in town," Mr. Reilly says. "And they don't have kids slandering me on the local news. Or stealing my avocados!"

"Let's just calm down, okay?" Mom says. "It's been a hard day. I'll talk to Peter."

That anger I felt this afternoon when I saw Mr. Reilly on his patio? I feel it again now, like a million little bolts of electricity are buzzing through my body and ricocheting off my bones. I'm all static, a firework about to launch.

Because if Mom is going to take someone's side, it should be mine. And there's nothing to apologize to Mr. Reilly for, anyway. I'm glad the world—or central Florida, at least—knows the truth about him now. Maybe he'll get arrested and he'll have to spend all his lottery money on bail and he won't be president of the Indigo River Boating Club anymore. That thought almost makes me smile. Almost.

But after Mr. Reilly leaves, Mom finds me in the hall and says, "Peter, you're grounded," and I'm definitely *not* smiling.

"I'm WHAT?"

"Marianne," Papa calls from the living room.

"Hang on, Dad," she yells. Her face is flushed and her

nostrils are flaring. "Peter, I specifically asked you not to cause trouble with Mr. Reilly—"

"I wasn't causing trouble! You didn't see the cut on Zoe's back. You don't understand—"

"What I understand is that you just accused Mr. Reilly with no proof—"

"Marianne," Papa calls again. "Come sit for a minute, love." He's trying to help me. I remind myself to thank him later.

"I don't need to sit, Dad!" she says. "I just need to—to—" I don't know what she needs to do because she doesn't finish that sentence. She just goes to her room and slams her door. The sound ripples like thunder through the house.

I know I should probably sit with Papa. Even if he seems fine right now—even if he's busy at work on hydropowered-lawnmower designs—he might get confused any second, especially with all this commotion. But if Mom gets to go to her room, then I should get to go to my room, too.

So I do. I go to my room and slam my door and practice drawing manatees in my sketchbook. When I press so hard that my pencil breaks, I find a new pencil.

I can't believe Mr. Reilly.

No—I can't believe *Mom*.

But honestly, who cares if I'm grounded? Wasn't I

already grounded? I already had to spend most of my summer at home with Papa, and there's no point going down to the canal now if Zoe is gone, and I'm not planning on spending any more time with people who are moving to Michigan. I'm not even *thinking* about people who are moving to Michigan.

While I draw manatee after manatee, I practice my not-thinking, because if you want to get really good at something, you should practice it a lot. I don't-think about the boxes in Tommy's room, stuffed with a thousand memories. I don't-think about the look on his face when he saw me standing in his house and how it made me want to yell and cry and hug him all at the same time. I don't-imagine my first day at Carter Middle School without him—walking the halls of a new school alone, sitting next to a stranger in class instead of the person who could never, ever be a stranger to me.

I practice my not-thinking so hard that I break another pencil. While I scrounge around for a fresh one on my desk, I hear Tommy's voice: "Peter, are you there?"

I freeze and stare at the walkie-talkie on my bedside table. I left it there after Tommy and I chatted late last night when I couldn't sleep.

"Peter, I know there's a ninety-seven percent chance you're really mad at me right now. Maybe a ninety-eight percent chance. But . . . please talk to me."

I pick up the walkie-talkie. It's heavy in my hands. Has it always been this heavy? My finger hovers over the talk button.

"Peter?"

No. I take out the batteries and bury the walkie-talkie at the bottom of my sock drawer. Maybe I'm being rude, but what's really rude is not telling your best friend that you're about to disappear forever.

Plus, we should get used to not using the walkie-talkies. They might be strong, but they're not Florida-to-Michigan strong.

I collapse onto my leaky beanbag chair with my sketchbook so I can keep drawing and not-thinking. I guess I get pretty focused because I jump when there's a knock on my door.

"I'm sleeping," I grumble.

The door opens and I stand up tall, ready to defend my rights of privacy, but it's not Mom.

"Papa, are you okay? Do you need your walker?"

He waves the suggestion away. "You know I hate that thing." One of his eyebrows lifts into an arch. It looks like a fuzzy caterpillar crawling across his face. "But what about you? Are *you* okay?"

His hand is holding tight to the doorknob and his left

leg is shaking, but his eyes are clear. They make me feel calm inside, like the world after a storm, when it's still raining a bit but the sun is out and everything is quiet and glittery. It's the same way I felt watching Zoe swim in the canal this past week.

Still, I'm not okay and he knows it.

"Marianne—your mom—she gets worked up sometimes. But she loves you. She's doing her best." He pauses. "For both of us."

I nod, then gulp. "Hey, Papa? What I said last night, about not having Tommy over . . ."

Papa raises a hand like he's in court and he's swearing to tell the whole truth and nothing but the truth. "Already forgotten." He laughs suddenly. "I'm forgetting a lot of things these days, aren't I?"

It's nice, hearing him laugh. It makes me laugh a little bit, too.

Still, I know he hasn't really forgotten. I also know an apology can't change what I said. I wish Papa could invent a time machine so I could go back and unsay it.

Actually, if I had a time machine, I could go back to the day Papa fell and hurt his hip. I could be there to stop it. To catch him.

Or I could go back even further, to before his dementia started, and figure out a way to prevent it.

Not having a time machine is a real bummer.

"What's this Emerald Springs place they mentioned on the news?" Papa asks.

Earlier, after Zoe was taken away, I found Papa standing by the living room window, staring out at the canal. Mom said he watched the whole rescue. She had tried to get him to sit down, but he wouldn't budge. Not till I got back home, at least.

"It's a state park," I say. "They have a manatee rehabilitation center there."

"If she comes back—*when* she comes back—I'll meet her. My legs, they're getting stronger. And your mom can't keep me in this house forever, can she?" He winks.

I know he's just trying to make me feel better. I decide to let him. "Sounds like a plan," I say.

When he goes back to the living room, I go with him. I sit on the floor by his recliner and show him my manatee drawings, and then he shows me *his* drawings, a.k.a. the latest hydropowered-lawnmower designs. They look a little squiggly to me, which is weird. Usually Papa's drawings are super sharp and careful.

"This one needs a name," he says. "Any ideas?"

I think about it for a minute. The Water Mower? No. Too easy. The Liquid Grass Chopper? No, that sounds too much like liquid grasshopper.

"Got it," I say. "The Aqua-Lawn-Chopper Deluxe!"

Papa starts writing the name above his design, then

pauses. "Can we call it deluxe if it's a first edition?"

"Yes," I say. "That's just good marketing. Everybody wants something deluxe."

"Ah," he says, writing *Deluxe.*

A little later, Mom comes out of her room and tells Papa it's bedtime.

"Not yet, love," he says.

I expect Mom to put up a fight, but she doesn't. She sits on the couch hugging a pillow to her chest, and we all watch *I Love Lucy,* Papa's favorite TV show of all time. It's the one where Lucy goes to a vineyard and stomps grapes with her bare feet. Papa and I have seen this one before—lots of times, actually—but we laugh like it's the first time. We laugh until Papa gets sleepy and closes his eyes. I grab the remote and turn down the volume.

"Peter?" Mom whispers. "I'm sorry. You're not grounded. I just . . ." She sighs. "It's been a lot lately. Hasn't it?"

I don't know what to say, but I look at her so she knows I'm listening. Her eyes are puffy.

"But we can handle a lot," she says. "We're a good team, you and me. Aren't we?"

I want to say *I don't know.* I want to say that sometimes it feels like we aren't on the same team at all.

But she needs me to say yes, so I do.

"I didn't know Tommy was moving, either," she says. "I would've told you. You know that, don't you? His parents didn't ask me to help them sell the house. Mr. Reilly made them an offer before they could even list it. I guess he wants the biggest house in the neighborhood."

"Mr. Reilly?" I hiss. Electricity crackles through my veins again, and memories flicker through my head—every time Mr. Reilly asked Tommy about the porch screening at his house; the way Mrs. Reilly smiled at us sadly. *It's hard, the way things change,* she said. *But that's life sometimes, isn't it?*

Ugh. Every time I think I can't hate him any more, Mr. Reilly finds a way to make me.

"I talked to Tommy's mom on the phone tonight," Mom says. "She thinks Tommy is really upset right now. He might not know how to say goodbye."

"It doesn't matter," I say, shaking my head, trying my hardest to mean it. "All that matters is that Zoe is okay. And Papa, too."

Mom gives me her I'm-worried-about-you look—crinkly forehead, a half frown—but I just close my eyes and rest my head on the arm of Papa's recliner. I'm tired. More tired than I've been in ages.

I guess I fall asleep like that because the next thing I know, the clock on the end table says it's three in the morning and Mom is sleeping on the couch, still clutching a pillow to her heart.

The TV is still on, too, except instead of *I Love Lucy*, it's the news. They're replaying the stories of the day, including

Zoe's rescue. And there I am again. *". . . and I know exactly who's to blame for hurting her."*

Papa laughs quietly, which surprises me. I thought he was asleep.

"You tell 'em," he says.

THIRTEEN

My goal for the second week of summer vacation: take
my caregiving skills to the next level. I might not have a
best friend anymore, or a Discovery Journal to complete,
or a manatee to check on, but that just means I can focus
completely on Papa. So I do.

Every day that Mom has to show houses or go into the
office, I give Papa his pills and make us peanut-butter-and-
jam (not jelly) sandwiches and corn chips for lunch. Well, I
don't make the corn chips, but I pour them out of the bag.
And when Papa takes his afternoon naps, I stick around
the house so I'm right there when he wakes up.

I must be doing a pretty fantastic job because for a few
days, Papa hardly gets confused at all. It almost feels normal,
like we actually *did* invent a time machine and we traveled

back to before Papa was sick. We watch *I Love Lucy* together and eat too much chocolate mint ice cream and work on new invention designs. Papa has an idea for how to motorize his walker and make it more fun to use.

But as hard as I try to focus on Papa, I can't stop thinking about Zoe. Papa can't, either. So we check the news a lot for updates. For a few days, Channel 9 repeats the footage of her rescue, but by the middle of the week, I guess they've moved on. Papa and I keep Channel 9 on all day, but there's not even one mention of Zoe.

"It's like they've totally forgotten about her!" I say, pointing at the TV with a blue ice pop. "It doesn't make sense. How do you forget a manatee? They're pretty unforgettable!"

"The news is fickle," Papa says.

I'm not sure what *fickle* means. I bet Tommy knows. Not that I'm thinking about Tommy. I'm becoming a not-thinking champion.

On Thursday afternoon, I check the Emerald Springs State Park website for news while Papa and I eat our PB&Js. I can't find anything about Zoe, which is just ridiculous. I'm busy searching the site for a phone number when the doorbell rings.

At first I wonder if it's Mr. Reilly coming to whine some more about me assassinating his character. But when I look through the peephole, I see the top of the head of a former best friend.

My heart starts jittering like it's tap-dancing inside my chest. He's not just a voice in my walkie-talkie—he's a real, live person on the other side of the door. His hair looks especially fluffy today. It must be the humidity.

I shake my head and put my foot down. Actually, my foot is already down, so I lift it and put it down again. I'm not opening the door. I have no idea what I'd say to Tommy, and just *thinking* about Tommy makes my eyes burn like someone poured sand in them. (I'm adding "losing friends" to the list of things that I'm allergic to.)

I stand by the door for a minute, real quiet, then check the peephole again. Tommy is walking away with his head down and his hands in the pockets of his cargo shorts. I blink a few times, because my allergies are being so stupid right now. So is my heart. I tell it to stop tap-dancing. It doesn't listen.

I head back to the kitchen. That's when I find Papa messing with the latches of the kitchen window.

"Papa, what're you doing?"

"The elevator's not working," he says hoarsely. "But they can't keep us here. I think we can get out this way."

My heart isn't dancing now. It's a big, heavy stone sinking down into the pit of my stomach. I thought I was doing a good job on Official Caregiver Duty. I thought I was helping his brain remember how to tick.

"Papa, we don't need to get out. This is home."

"There's still time, but we have to hurry. Get Marianne. Ask her to bring my toolkit."

I take deep breaths while Papa's shaking hands fumble with the latches. Those latches are super easy to unlock. I've done it plenty of times. But he can't seem to figure it out.

I place a hand on his arm, thinking fast. "I was just about to call Emerald Springs to check on Zoe."

"Zoe," Papa says slowly, like the name is new—like he's testing it out—even though we were just talking about her a few minutes ago.

"The manatee," I say. "I bet she'll be back soon, and you'll be able to meet her. I can tell that your legs are getting stronger! And maybe . . . maybe we can invent something for her. Something awesome. We can make it together. That'd be fun, wouldn't it?"

It's quiet. Papa stands at the window, staring at the latches. His arm trembles under my hand. I can't tell if he's still confused or if he *knows* he was just confused and he's embarrassed. And I wonder what it feels like, to know your mind just went somewhere strange and to not know when you might go to that place again. To not be able to control it. To not be able to *fix* it when you're supposed to be able to fix anything.

Finally, Papa nods and sits back down. Whew.

I find the number for Emerald Springs, but I just get an

automated message. So much for that plan.

But then, after lunch, when Papa lies down for his nap, I come up with plan B and dial another number.

"Thanks for calling the Florida Manatee Society, central Florida's longest-running manatee research and—"

"Hi, Cassidy Cawley. It's me."

"Um, who's me? I mean, who's you?"

"Peter. We met last weekend when you came to my neighborhood to help Zoe—"

"Peter! Hey, do you know that video of you pointing at your neighbor has over a thousand views on YouTube?"

"That's not very impressive," I say. "There's a video of two eastern gray squirrels wrestling over a nut that has over a million views."

"Oh, I *love* that video! But what I'm saying is, you're kind of famous. Like, locally." She pauses. "Although, we're all kind of famous these days, aren't we?"

I pace the living room the way Mom does when she's on the phone with her clients. "Are the people who are watching the video mad at Mr. Reilly? Is he going to jail?"

"I think the people watching the video just think you're . . . I don't know. A cute and funny kid."

Well, it's nice to be cute and funny, but I'd like it better if Mr. Reilly was going to jail. "Listen," I say. "I need to know how Zoe's doing, and if she's coming back, and when she's coming back."

"Oh," says Cassidy. "Well, I don't know much yet. She's at the manatee rehabilitation center at Emerald Springs State Park. But hey, I'm driving down there on Sunday to check on her! I know a guy there who—well, he's just a friend. A guy-friend. Did I already tell you about him?" I don't have to see her to know that she's blushing. "Anyway, I could give you an update after that."

I run back to the kitchen and check Mom's work schedule, which is pinned to the fridge beneath a seashell magnet. Looks like she's not working on Sunday, which means I won't be on caregiver duty. "Can I come with you?"

"Well . . . I guess you *could*," says Cassidy. "I mean, if your mom and dad are okay with it."

"I don't have a dad."

"Oh!"

"I mean, I *do* have a dad, but he lives in North Carolina, so it's kind of like he doesn't exist."

"Peter, I'm sorry—"

"So can I have my mom call you?"

"Sure!" says Cassidy. She's probably relieved she doesn't have to come up with something to say about Dad being gone. This happens a lot. "Does your friend Tommy want to come, too?"

"I don't have any friends named Tommy," I say, and then I hang up.

When Mom gets home, I tell her to call the Florida

Manatee Society tomorrow between the business hours of nine a.m. and five p.m. so she can talk to Cassidy and decide it's safe for me to go to the manatee rehabilitation center at Emerald Springs State Park on Sunday so I can check on Zoe and make sure she's okay, and then give Papa an update, which might help him feel better and be less confused. But I guess I say it all too fast, because she says, "Slow down, slow down!" So I try again, more slowly this time.

"I don't think so, Peter," she says, riffling through her briefcase. "I'm worried you're thinking too much about that manatee."

"How can you think too much about a manatee?"

"Ugh, where is that contract for the Harleys?!" She upends her briefcase over the kitchen table and starts poring through a bunch of boring-looking papers.

I think Mom is like the Channel 9 news. She just wants to move on. But I'm not moving on. I ask her over and over again if I can go to Emerald Springs with Cassidy. People like to say the third time's the charm. I don't know about that. I have to ask Mom to call Cassidy at least seventeen times, but eventually her "no" becomes a "Dear God, Peter, what's the number?"

She calls the Florida Manatee Society on Friday morning and I decide that I'm very persuasive.

FOURTEEN

Riding in Cassidy's tiny green car is like riding an old, rickety roller coaster. It's bumpy and noisy, and my stomach flips every time we turn.

"What's wrong with your car?" I ask.

"There's nothing *wrong* with it. I mean, it won't stop veering to the left. And I don't know what that smell is. But I'm going to get it fixed up soon."

She's right. There is a funky smell. I press a button to turn up the fans.

"I'm going to drive an Aston Martin someday," I say. I don't know a whole lot about cars, but I saw a really sweet-looking car in a movie once and I asked Papa what it was and he said it was an Aston Martin.

We lurch to a stop in front of a red light. "Wow," says

Cassidy. "What kind of job are you gonna have to afford an Aston Martin?"

"Me and Tommy, we're going—" I pause. It's hard work pretending someone doesn't exist. You have to cut them out of every memory *and* every future you've ever imagined. *"I'm* going to be an animal discoverer. I'm going to find new animals, and name them, and some of them will probably be named after me."

Even as I say it, though, I wonder if it's still true. Can I be an animal discoverer if Tommy isn't there to help? He's always been the researcher.

"That sounds fun," says Cassidy. The light turns green. She steps on the gas, and the car shudders back to life. "Though, I'm not sure animal discoverers can afford Aston Martins."

"I'm going to draw the animals, too," I say.

"Oh," says Cassidy. I think she understands now.

When we merge onto the highway, Cassidy yelps and grips the steering wheel so hard her knuckles turn white.

"Are you okay?" I ask.

"I hate merging," she says.

"Cassidy Cawley, are you neurotic?"

"No! I mean, maybe. But everyone is neurotic, right? Who taught you that word, anyway?"

"Tommy," I say, then clamp my mouth shut.

She gives me a sideways glance. "I thought you didn't

have any friends named Tommy."

"Hey," I say, "how many manatees have you met?"

This is called *diverting*. It's a technique I learned from Mom. She used to take me to house showings with her sometimes when I was younger. Whenever her client would say something like, "Maybe we shouldn't move after all," Mom would say, "Have you *seen* these gorgeous crown moldings?" Bam! Diverted.

It works like a charm on Cassidy. "Hmm, I don't know," she says. "Dozens, I guess? In college, I spent a couple months studying them in Key West. That's where I met Billy."

"Billy?"

"My friend who works at Emerald Springs. My guy-friend. The friend who's a guy." She inspects her reflection in the rearview and tucks a loose strand of hair behind her ear.

"And now you work for the Florida Manatee Society?"

She nods. "I spent my summers interning with them during college. When I graduated last month, Maria, the president, offered me a full-time job, which . . . Honestly, I can't believe it. Maria and her whole team are amazing. They know so much. When they talk about the work they do, they sound so—" She sighs. The car sighs with her. "Assured."

We hit another red light. Cassidy rolls her shoulders

back and sits a little taller. "It's good. I mean, I just started, but . . . it's good. I love working directly with animals, but I'm excited to learn more about animal advocacy, too."

"What's animal advocacy?" If Tommy was here, I bet he would know. But I don't need Tommy. I've got Cassidy.

"You know, like . . . fighting for laws and stuff to protect animals. That's what Maria has done her whole life."

I think about this. "Are there laws that will make Mr. Reilly go to jail?"

"Hmm. I don't know. And we don't really have any proof that he's the one who hit her."

"Zoe was right by his dock! And you should hear the way he talks about manatees. It's awful. He doesn't think they matter. He doesn't think anything matters besides himself."

Cassidy looks at me. I can't tell what she's thinking. I don't like not knowing what people are thinking.

"I found the video of me on YouTube," I say. "It has almost two thousand views now, but I don't like the comments. Nobody is taking me seriously."

"Word to the wise," says Cassidy. "Never read the comments. Actually, just stay off the internet."

I have more questions I want to ask, about advocacy and laws and what's wrong with the internet, but she connects her phone to the car's speakers and suddenly we're listening to a podcast about nuclear fission, of all things.

Then I realize it's actually a *Science Daily* episode, which, of course, makes me think about—

I turn off the radio. "I like silence," I say, which isn't true but is right now.

So we drive in silence until we pass the sign for Emerald Springs State Park and it's time to unmerge.

"Are you going to yelp again?"

"No," says Cassidy.

Still, she yelps a little bit when we unmerge. I yelp a little bit, too, so she doesn't feel alone. Feeling alone is the worst.

Then we're on a quiet road surrounded by trees, and a few minutes later we're pulling into the parking lot of Emerald Springs State Park.

I'm feeling bouncy. I think it's because I'm about to see Zoe. Cassidy looks bouncy, too. I think it's because she's about to see Billy.

Before we get out of the car, I call Mom to let her know we made it.

"Thank God," she says.

When Cassidy came to pick me up, Mom talked to her for a few minutes, but I think Mom is still worried about me hanging out with a "stranger," which is kind of annoying but also kind of nice. Mom's so worried about Papa these days that it's nice to know she still has some worries left over for me.

"Be careful," Mom says. "Keep your phone on. And drink water! The high today is ninety-nine degrees."

Just as she says that, Cassidy and I step out of the car and the sun punches me right in the face. Not literally, but . . . kind of literally.

Mom doesn't need to remind me to drink water, though. "Stay Hydrated" is one of the rules of the Discovery Club.

Not that the Discovery Club exists anymore.

FIFTEEN

I can't believe I've never been to Emerald Springs State Park before. There are animals *everywhere*. There's an alligator lagoon, a hippopotamus pool, and a bobcat enclosure, plus some whooping cranes and flamingos. There's even a couple of black bears. And a panther! When I see the panther, I get so excited I feel dizzy. Or maybe that's just the heat.

But I feel sort of sad, too. "Do the animals ever get to leave the park?" I ask Cassidy.

"Well . . . no," she says. "But these animals are here because they can't survive in the wild, so it's a little different than a normal zoo. It's more like a retirement community. Most of these guys have pretty bad injuries."

Well, that just makes me sadder.

The manatee rehabilitation center at the back of the park is closed to the public, but I guess not to Florida Manatee Society members, because Cassidy slips past the Employees Only sign. I follow her. If anybody asks, I'm going to say I work at the Florida Manatee Society, too. Maybe I'm Cassidy's assistant. Or maybe I'm her boss.

The center is way smaller than I imagined. I thought it would be a giant aquarium with nice music playing for the manatees, and they'd be selling manatee stuffed animals and maybe some ice pops or churros, too. But it's actually just a couple of pools and some big pumps and lots of pipes, which is a bummer. I don't like the idea of Zoe being stuck here.

The only person at the center is a guy tossing heads of lettuce into one of the pools. He's tall and lean, dressed in all khaki—khaki shorts, khaki button-up shirt, and I'm pretty sure his sunhat is khaki, too. When he sees us approaching, he grins. "Cassidy!" He tries to give Cassidy a handshake while Cassidy tries to give him a hug, and they both say "Oh!" and it's one of the most awkward things I've ever seen.

"Peter, this is Billy," Cassidy says. "Billy, Peter. He's the one who reported the manatee that was brought in last weekend."

"Peter! I've seen you on YouTube, buddy. You're going viral!"

I shrug. I'm going to need a lot more views if I'm going to compete with those two squirrels fighting over a nut.

"Billy and I studied manatees in Key West together in college," says Cassidy. "I mean, he was in grad school, and I was just an undergrad, but . . . Anyway, now he works here at Emerald Springs!"

"Guilty as charged," Billy says.

He says some other things, too, but I'm not really listening. I'm looking into the pool where Billy was tossing the lettuce. Three manatees—two big ones and a smaller one—are munching on romaine with their funny vacuum-like mouths. I get a full head-to-toe shiver. A couple weeks ago I had never seen a manatee before, and now I'm seeing *three*. Three giant blobs. Three gray islands.

But none of them have a Z-shaped cut.

"Where's Zoe?" I ask.

"Zoe?" says Billy.

"The new manatee," says Cassidy. "That's what Peter calls her."

"Ah! She's over there in our isolation pool."

Isolation. I don't like the sound of that. I run to the smaller pool, where just one manatee is floating silently through the water. There's the Z, and there's the new cut, more pink than red now but still awful.

"Zoe," I whisper, because it feels like a time for whispering. It's so nice to see her.

"She's a trooper," Billy says.

"Why is she by herself?"

"She was in bad shape when she got here. She had a punctured lung, and that cut was infected. When they come in really sick like that, especially when there's an infection, we have to separate them from the others."

A punctured lung. I feel a fresh wave of rage toward Mr. Reilly. "Is she going to be okay?"

Billy takes a handkerchief out of his pocket and mops the sweat off his brow. "When she first got here," he says, "she couldn't move at all. But she's starting to swim around a bit. She still doesn't want to eat solid food, but we're giving her liquid food injections. For now, though, it's mostly watch and wait."

"Watch and wait for what?" I say, but I already know and Billy doesn't answer.

While I sit by the pool, Billy and Cassidy find a shady spot nearby and chat. I hear Billy tell Cassidy that the center is planning on building a new state-of-the-art pool to increase their capacity for injured manatees. Cassidy tells Billy that the Florida Manatee Society is planning on attending an Indigo River Boating Club meeting later this summer to share manatee safety tips with the boaters.

Part of me wants to join them in the shade—99 degrees might as well be 450 degrees—but I don't want to leave Zoe. She drifts toward me and her beady eyes meet mine, and even though I'm worried to death about her, I feel it again—a quiet stillness inside me, like someone just turned down the volume on the world and I can breathe more easily. I know she's hurt, but she looks so peaceful in the water.

I have a sudden urge to jump into the pool, to float next to her and let the water hold me the way it's holding her. But I know that's probably against Emerald Springs rules, so I just sit as close to the pool as I can.

"Do you remember me?" I whisper.

Zoe doesn't answer, of course. But I swear her eyes shine a little brighter.

I don't know how long I sit there. All I know is that it feels like waking from a dream when Cassidy says, "Ready to go?"

"Five more minutes," I say.

When those five minutes are up, I ask for five more, even though I might pass out if I spend another second in the sun. Because as long as I'm watching Zoe, I know she's okay. And somehow, if Zoe is okay, maybe everything else is okay, too.

But then Billy says it's time for Zoe's next injection, and I really don't want to see that. So I agree to go—on one condition. "Can I come back soon?"

"You're welcome back anytime, buddy," says Billy. "I'm here most days of the week."

"You should really update the Emerald Springs website, too," I say. "Maybe you can start a blog about Zoe."

Billy laughs. "I'll pass along the recommendation." Then he tries to hug Cassidy, but this time she tries to just shake his hand, and it's somehow even more awkward than the first time.

"See you soon," I whisper to Zoe.

I follow Cassidy out of the manatee center, looking back over my shoulder only about twenty times. Cassidy looks over her shoulder a few times, too, but I don't think it's for Zoe.

On our walk back through the park, my whole body feels heavy. I'm pretty sure the heat is multiplying gravity right now. My mouth is parched, too, and that's when I realize that I forgot to stay hydrated. It's hard to remember the rules of a club that doesn't exist anymore.

Before we leave Emerald Springs State Park, we stop by the gift shop for water bottles, but I get distracted by the manatee key chains.

"Do you want one?" Cassidy says.

"Yes," I say with all of my being.

I pick out one that says "Mana-Tea Time!" It's a manatee drinking tea. I giggle. Cassidy giggles, too. I decide that she might be new-best-friend material.

"Don't *ever* move to Michigan," I tell her.

SIXTEEN

The drive home feels twice as long, probably because Cassidy and I don't say much. We listen to the hit songs of yesterday and today on the radio and yelp when we merge, but otherwise it's quiet.

I look out at the palm trees and shrubs that line the highway, passing by so fast that they all blur into a wall of green-brown, and the heat shimmering like magic on the road ahead of us. We never catch up to the shimmer.

"Hey, Cassidy Cawley?"

"Why do you keep using my full name?"

"You have one of those names that sounds nice all together. Like George Washington."

She turns down the music. "Well, we call him George Washington. But his friends probably didn't call him

George Washington, right?"

"What else would they have called him?"

"I'm just saying, you can call me Cassidy, if you want."

I think about this. "No," I say. "Hey, Cassidy Cawley?"

She laughs. "Yeah?"

"When is the Indigo River Boating Club meeting? The one that the Florida Manatee Society is going to?"

"The end of July."

"I want to go."

"Oh," says Cassidy. "Um, I don't think that meeting will be super fun, Peter. The Florida Manatee Society has tried to work with the boating club before, and Maria says it can be a tough crowd."

I picture a crowd full of Mr. Reillys. It's not a pretty sight.

"But I'm sort of internet famous now, right? So, I can help. Maybe I can give a speech! I give great speeches."

Cassidy takes her eyes off the road long enough to gawk at me. "Wait—you mean you actually *want* to talk to a room full of people? Maria wants me to speak, but I *hate* public speaking."

"I could take your place!"

She sighs. "I wish. Maria says talking at the meeting will be good experience for me, even though there are other people on our team who would be *way* better, and who know so much more than I do, and—" Her knuckles turn white again as she clenches the wheel. "I think I have to do it."

"Why don't we both speak?" I say, because this is the obvious solution.

"Well . . . maybe. I mean, if Maria is on board, and you clear it with your mom——"

"I'm so glad we could come to an arrangement," I say, which is a phrase I picked up from Mom. It's what she says when house sellers and house buyers agree on a price.

Cassidy looks at me funny. Maybe she doesn't speak real estate lingo. But then a car honks at her and she jumps and glues her eyes on the road.

"The car keeps drifting," she mutters.

I decide that I'm going to buy Cassidy a new car when I'm older and I have a lot of money as the world's greatest animal discoverer.

I also decide that I'm going to the Indigo River Boating Club meeting, where I will give an inspirational speech that will make everyone realize that we all need to work together to save the manatees. While I'm making my speech, I'm going to look right at Mr. Reilly, and he won't be able to slam a door in my face. He'll have to listen to me.

Then, once Zoe is better—and she *will* get better—it'll be safe for her to move back into the canal, because all the boaters will have to drive at slower speeds and do other safe things.

Then, once Zoe is back, I'll take Papa down to the canal to meet her. Maybe seeing her will help him feel better. Maybe it'll clear his head, the way it clears mine. And then Mom won't have to stop working when I go back to school.

That's the plan. It's a pretty sweet plan, and if I follow it, everything will go back to normal.

Well, except for Tommy, but I'm still not-thinking about him. The not-thinking is tough—every time I try, I feel a pain in my chest, like my heart is a lemon and someone is juicing it—but I'll keep at it. Practice makes perfect.

"Which house is it again?" Cassidy asks when we pull into my neighborhood.

"The small one with the blue door."

Her car shrieks like a banshee as she hits the brake.

"Thank you," I say. "For the trip. And the key chain."

"Anytime! Well, not anytime. I don't go to Emerald Springs every day. But, like, sometimes."

As I'm getting out of the car, she says, "Hey, Peter? Don't stop discovering and drawing animals. Even if it doesn't make you rich. I mean, money is nice. But it's not everything. So don't stop. Okay?"

"Okay," I say, even though I'm pretty sure it *will* make me rich, especially because now I won't have to split all the money I earn with Tommy.

I give Cassidy a wave as she drives away, then head inside. I know something fishy is going on as soon as I step foot in the house because I hear Mr. and Mrs. Saunders talking to Mom in the kitchen.

"—heard you were taking a break from real estate, and we didn't know whether to ask you—" Mr. Saunders is saying.

Then Mrs. Saunders: "Eddie made an offer on the house on the spot. With my job starting so soon in Michigan, we had to move fast—"

"Really, it's okay," says Mom. "I understand."

They fall silent when I walk into the kitchen.

"Peter," Mom says. She smiles and nods toward the living room. "Tommy's here to see you. Isn't that nice?"

Mr. and Mrs. Saunders smile, too. Three too-wide smiles, all pointed at me.

My insides churn as I walk slowly into the living room. The ground feels unsteady beneath my feet, like a ship on rough waves. Is it possible to be seasick on land?

There's Papa in his recliner, watching *I Love Lucy*. And there, sitting on the couch, is Tommy, wearing his favorite NASA T-shirt and wriggling like a fish on a hook. He stands when he sees me. "Peter," he says.

"Tommy," I say. My heart starts tap-dancing again.

"I was wondering if we could—if I could—" He sneezes. "Could we talk?"

No. This isn't right. This isn't supposed to be happening. The plan was to forget Tommy. Doesn't he have any respect for the plan?

I look at the front door. I want to run—out of the house, out of the neighborhood, maybe all the way back to Emerald Springs. But Mom and Tommy's parents are all staring at me, smiling. Waiting. I feel like an animal in a cage.

Fine. If I can't run, I'll just have to stand my ground. While Tommy keeps fidgeting, I think up a whole bunch of different ways to tell him to leave and never come back. Some of them are pretty epic. Some of them use words that I'm not allowed to say, but if there was ever a time to say them, this is it, right?

But then I look at Papa. He isn't staring at me like Mom or Mr. and Mrs. Saunders. He isn't silently begging me to act super happy or give Tommy a big hug. He's clear-eyed and looking at me like he knows this is hard, but he knows I can handle it, too.

He gives me a smile—it's small but it's real—and a nod.

I turn back to Tommy. "Okay," I say. "Let's talk."

SEVENTEEN

Tommy wanted to talk but he isn't doing any talking. He's just sitting in my desk chair, staring at the carpet and sniffling. I'm in my beanbag chair. It's leaking beans.

I check my solar system watch. According to the planetary alignment of Jupiter and Earth, we've been sitting here in silence for four minutes now. It feels like eons, though. I'm starting to think we might just grow old and die right here, but then Tommy finally opens his mouth—

—and closes it.

He does this a few times—open, closed, open, closed—until I say, "Good grief! Say *something*!"

"Peter, I'm really sorry I didn't tell you we were moving

or that Mr. Reilly bought our house." He blurts it out so fast that it all sounds like one long, weird word. It takes my brain a few seconds to insert the right spaces and make sense of it.

"I tried to, a few times," he says. "But I was afraid you might get"—he glances at me, then away—"mad."

Oh boy. The fact that Tommy didn't tell me he was moving because he thought I might get mad *really* makes me mad!

Fighting to keep my voice steady, I say, "But *why* are you moving? And when did you find out? And is this a temporary thing or is it for good?" There's so much more I want to ask. All the questions that I've been not-thinking for the past week are bubbling up now and spilling out of me. But I start with these so I don't overwhelm Tommy. He's already squirming.

"My mom got an offer to be an astronomy professor at the University of Michigan," he says. Then, a little quieter, "A couple of months ago."

"A COUPLE OF MONTHS! That means there were, like, a *billion* times when you could have told me! This whole time we've been hanging out, and talking about middle school, you *knew* you were moving. You *knew* you wouldn't be there with me."

He sniffs and looks away. When he speaks again, his voice is shaky, like each word is walking a tightrope. "I don't *want* to go to Michigan, Peter. I don't want to go any-where. At first I didn't tell you because I thought maybe it wasn't true, even when my parents accepted Mr. Reilly's offer to buy our house. It didn't make sense to tell you until I was a hundred percent sure it was happening, not just eighty-seven percent sure, or ninety-three percent sure. But now that we're moving in two weeks—"

"TWO WEEKS!"

Tommy slumps a little lower in my chair. "We're driving to Michigan the last weekend of June."

The beanbag wheezes as I stand and start pacing my room. I don't look at Tommy. I *can't* look at Tommy.

"Can you even *drive* to Michigan?" I ask. I don't know where Michigan is, exactly—Tommy's the one who's good at geography, not me—but I know it isn't close.

"It'll take two days. We're stopping in Nashville on the way."

"NASHVILLE!" I don't know why I yell this. I don't know anything about Nashville. But right now the idea of Tommy going to another strange place is more than I can bear.

"Country music capital of the world," he mumbles. And then he starts to cry.

This isn't the first time Tommy has cried in front of me. He cried when we were running away from that alligator, and when he got his foot stuck under that tree root in the swamp, and when Mr. Reilly caught us stealing avocados. Some other times, too.

The weird thing is, Tommy doesn't wipe away his tears when he cries. He just lets them run down his face, and his nose runs, too, so his face gets all wet and goopy. And the worst part? You never know how long it'll last. Jupiter could make a hundred trips around the sun, and Tommy will still be crying.

Actually, the worst part is that watching Tommy cry makes *my* eyes start to burn. I think I'm allergic to other people crying. I'm allergic to so much these days.

I shut my eyes tight to make the burning go away, except that it doesn't, and with my eyes shut, all the questions in my head get louder.

Like, how am I supposed to go to Carter Middle School without Tommy?

And is this really the end of the Discovery Club?

And what's going to happen to the journal?

And is Tommy going to leave without even knowing that Papa has Alzheimer's?

This was way easier when I was so mad at Tommy that I could pretend there wasn't a Tommy, that there had never *been* a Tommy. But now there *is* a Tommy and he's sitting right in front of me and I *am* mad but I'm also a lot of other things and I don't know how to focus on one thing at a time because I don't even know what all the things are.

I sit on the edge of my bed and squeeze my hands together and breathe. "I saw Zoe today," I say, because if I say something, maybe I won't combust. I feel like a bean-bag chair trying to hold in all my beans.

"Your mom told me," Tommy says between hiccups. He always hiccups when he cries. "How is she?"

"It's watch and wait," I say, even though I hate those words. "But the Florida Manatee Society is speaking at an Indigo River Boating Club meeting at the end of July, and I'm going to go and make an inspirational speech and convince all the boaters to help protect manatees so what happened to Zoe doesn't happen again."

It feels good to say it. It feels good to talk about something that isn't Tommy leaving.

"And this is a *secret*," I say. "If Mom finds out I'm going to do something that might tick off Mr. Reilly, she won't let me go."

"Wow," says Tommy, his voice thick with tears. "What're you going to say to the boaters?"

"Well . . . I don't know yet. But I'll think of something. Something amazing. Something life-changing."

Tommy knuckles snot away from his nose. "You'll need research. And data. Pertinent data."

"Well, duh," I say, because of course I'll need pertinent data, whatever *pertinent* means.

"*Science Daily* did an episode on the psychology of persuasion," Tommy says. He's still crying, but he sounds excited now, too. "They talked about the importance of building a watertight case. Or, at least, a case that *seems* watertight."

"My case really *will* be watertight," I say. "And . . ." I look at him. I take another breath. "You're going to help me build it."

Tommy blinks. "I am?"

I'm as surprised as he is. More surprised, probably. What on earth or Jupiter am I saying? Why would I want Tommy's help after he kept the truth from me for so long?

But there's an idea brewing in my head. It must've started in my subconscious brain—the subconscious is sneaky like that—but now it's in my conscious brain and I can see it. I can hold it. It might just be my best idea ever.

"T-minus two weeks?"

Tommy nods. "T-minus two"—hiccup—"weeks."

"Then we have two weeks to build a watertight case to convince the boaters to help the manatees." I sound very impressive when I say this, like someone who decides to do things and then does them.

"But, Peter, if Mr. Reilly finds out—"

"What's he going to do?"

"He still owes my parents money for the house. He could back out, or—or—get us both in trouble again!"

I think about what Mom said. *Mr. Reilly isn't a good person to upset.* But I'm not afraid of him. I've never been afraid of him.

Also, he's my archnemesis. It's my job to upset him.

"I'm doing this," I say. "I *have* to do this." I stand and offer Tommy my hand. "So what do you say, Fox? Are you in?"

Tommy looks at my hand. For a few long seconds, it's totally silent. Well, besides all of his sniffling and hiccupping. My outstretched arm is just hanging there, and I'm beginning to wonder if he *isn't* in, when he finally stands, smiles, and takes my hand. "I'm in, Falcon."

His hand is kind of snotty, which is super gross. But his smile makes me feel better, like things are already getting back to normal. Like my secret plan is already working.

The secret plan goes like this: If I can keep Tommy busy helping me prepare for the boating club meeting, maybe—just *maybe*—he'll realize that he can't go to Michigan. That his life is here, working with me, helping to save the world. His parents will see it, too. They'll see he belongs here. With me.

It's a way better plan than trying to forget Tommy.

Because if this plan works, I won't need to forget.

Also, it makes my heart feel a little less like an over-squeezed lemon.

I give Tommy's hand a good shake. "Game on," I say.

"Game"—hiccup—"on."

EIGHTEEN

Even after finishing Zoe's entry in the Discovery Journal, Tommy and I still have a lot to learn about West Indian manatees—especially if we're going to build a watertight case for why boaters should help protect them.

It turns out that back in the 1970s, way before Tommy or I were born, West Indian manatees almost totally disappeared from the planet, which is hard to even imagine. If manatees had gone extinct, I would never have met Zoe. I wouldn't have met Cassidy or Billy, either. The Florida Manatee Society wouldn't even exist!

But luckily, a bunch of animal activists and conservationists worked really hard to save the West Indian manatee, and now there are thousands of them swimming around Florida. It's pretty amazing.

Manatees still face tons of threats, though, and they could still go extinct. In fact, the West Indian manatee is classified as "vulnerable to extinction" by the International Union for the Conservation of Nature, a.k.a. the IUCN.

Humans cause a lot of manatee deaths, mainly by hitting them with boats, the way Mr. Reilly almost definitely hit Zoe. But there are lots of things boaters can do to help manatees, like obeying speed zone signs posted in waterways, and staying in deep-water channels (manatees usually stick to shallow water), and not throwing trash in the water.

Also, boaters can wear polarized sunglasses, which remove the sun's glare when you look at the water, so it's easier to see if there are manatees swimming around you.

"How do you spell *polarized*?" I say.

"*P-O-L-A-R-I-Z-E-D*," says Tommy.

He's researching manatee conservation tips on his computer, and I'm writing down the important stuff on a poster we dug out of his closet. The poster was part of Tommy's fourth-grade science fair project on light refraction, whatever that is, so I'm making my manatee poster on the back.

"It says here that boaters should report injured manatees immediately to the Florida Marine—"

"Slow down!" I say. "I'm still writing *polarized*." I'm usually a fast writer, but right now I'm writing in block letters with markers, and each letter gets a different color, because visual aids should be eye-catching.

It was my idea to make a visual aid for my speech at the Indigo River Boating Club meeting. When you're talking to a room full of people and you want to seem official and important, it's good to be able to point to something. Tommy suggested making a slideshow on his computer, but I don't know if there will be a projector at the meeting, and Tommy was just going to toss his old science fair poster, anyway. His parents told him to "pare down" his stuff as he packs.

And boy, is he packing. I've been coming to Tommy's house every evening this week after Mom gets home from work, and I swear the cardboard boxes just keep multiplying. It's almost like Tommy is *actually* about to move. Every time I look at those boxes, the room spins like the Gravitron at the state fair and I feel seasick again.

But I still have nine days to make him realize he has to stay. A lot can happen in nine days, especially nine long summer days. It's basically an eternity.

"What was that about reporting an injury?" I say.

"Boaters should report injured manatees immediately to the Florida Marine Life Commission by calling eight-eight-eight—"

"Hold on, hold on!" Tommy doesn't understand that you can't rush block letters.

While I'm lettering, he spins around in his wheelie

chair. "Could we work on this at your house instead?"

"You know we can't. We have to keep this a secret from my mom."

"I know. But I was just thinking that maybe tomorrow, when your mom is at work—"

I shake my head. "Too risky."

Tommy nods. "I just don't like my room much right now," he mumbles. I wonder if he's about to cry again. Ever since we talked at my house last weekend, he's been randomly bursting into tears. It's really been messing with my allergies.

The truth is, I don't like Tommy's room much right now, either. But I still haven't told Tommy about Papa being sick or how I'm on Official Caregiver Duty this summer.

It's not that Tommy would be weird or mean about Papa's dementia. He'd probably be super nice about it. It's just . . . well, if Papa is going to get better soon, then I don't *need* to tell anyone about his dementia. Telling Tommy about it would just make it a bigger thing, and I don't think I can stand it feeling any bigger than it already does.

So for now, as much as I hate watching Tommy's whole life disappear into boxes, his house is headquarters for our watertight case-building.

And it's not *all* bad over here. Mr. and Mrs. Saunders bring us lots of snacks and orange soda, and every time they pop in, they get to see how much fun we're having.

They get to see that Tommy belongs here.

"Okay," I say, "what's the rest of the Marine Life Commission number?"

When I finish writing the number—each digit gets a different color—I wait for Tommy to give me another fact to add to the poster, but he doesn't. He just spins in circles in his wheelie chair, round and round. "I think we've covered the main things boaters should know."

I look at the poster's blank spaces and frown. "I could fit at least five more facts on here."

"Maybe you could draw pictures in the empty spaces?"

That's not a bad idea. I've been drawing manatees for weeks now, and I've gotten pretty great at it.

But I've got an even better idea. A way to learn more about manatee conservation *and* remind Tommy how awesome and un-leave-able Florida is.

"Tommy," I say, "it's time for us to visit Emerald Springs State Park."

NINETEEN

I forgot to warn Tommy about Cassidy's dying car. He sits beside me in the back seat in wide-eyed terror as the car groans like some kind of monster from the deep. When we merge onto the highway and Cassidy yelps, he digs his fingers into my arm.

"Ow!"

He loosens his grip but doesn't let go. "There's a *Science Daily* episode about the physiology of fear," he says. "I think I'm experiencing all of the symptoms."

"I love *Science Daily*!" says Cassidy. "Have you heard the one about octopus intelligence? They're SO smart. It's kind of scary."

Yesterday I called Cassidy and learned that Maria Liu, her boss, loves the idea of me speaking at the Indigo River

Boating Club meeting next month. I told her that Mom was okay with it, too, which is a lie. I don't like lying, but I figure this one is okay because it's for a good cause. Also, according to Tommy, some people think morality is relative. I don't know what that means, really, except that it was maybe okay for me to lie to Cassidy.

Then I asked Cassidy if she would take me and Tommy to Emerald Springs State Park today so we could ask her and Billy some questions about manatee conservation for my speech to the boating club. She said, "I thought you didn't have any friends named Tommy," and I said, "Try to keep up."

So, here Tommy and I are, in the back seat of Cassidy's car, on a mission to build the most watertight case ever.

Well, that's the main mission. There's also the secret mission—to show Tommy that there are parts of Florida he hasn't even *seen* yet. I mean, who could move to Michigan after seeing Emerald Springs State Park?

When we get to the park, I pretend I'm an official Emerald Springs tour guide. "We'll begin our tour at the bobcat enclosure," I say in what feels like a tour guide sort of voice—loud and singsong-y. A few strangers stare at me. I don't care. They can join the tour if they want.

"Um, Peter, I thought we were here to talk to Billy," says Cassidy.

"We are," I say. "Just as soon as I show Tommy everything." I want to say, *You can wait a few more minutes to see your crush*, but I don't. I'm a very restrained person when I put my mind to it.

"Peter, this is *amazing*," says Tommy when we reach the first tour stop. "I was just reading an article about bobcats. They're nocturnal, so they're rarely spotted in the wild. Did you know they're excellent swimmers? Everyone thinks cats hate swimming, but that's not always true . . ." His eyes are wide, and he's talking so fast he trips over the words. So far, the secret mission is an epic success.

After the bobcat enclosure, I drag Tommy down every path, showing him the whooping cranes and the rhinoceros and the panther. He takes lots of notes and pictures on his phone. He even takes pictures of the signs around the park that have descriptions of the animals and maps of where they can be found in the wild.

We pause by the hippopotamus enclosure long enough to watch the hippo lumber down into a pond. While Tommy takes pictures, I lace my fingers through the diamond-shaped holes of the fence.

"You know," he says, "if these animals counted as discoveries, we could probably finish the journal today."

He's right. He's even got the journal right there in his backpack. And it's tempting. We're *so close* to finishing it, especially since we found a six-spotted tiger beetle on my flip-flop the other day (Discovery #97).

But there's no rush. There will be plenty of time later this summer, once Tommy and his family decide to stay forever.

"We can't break the rules of the Discovery Club," I remind him. "No captive animals."

"What's the Discovery Club?" says Cassidy, spooking me. I'd forgotten she was behind us.

Tommy and I look at each other, a question in our eyes. We usually don't talk about the Discovery Club to anyone who isn't in the club, meaning anyone who isn't us. Well, except for our parents, who have to drive us places to see animals. And Papa. I've told Papa all about it.

But I like Cassidy enough to let her in on the secret. I nod to Tommy and he pulls out the journal.

"The purpose of the Discovery Club is to fill the Discovery Journal, a catalog of every animal species we can find in the wild," I say. "Every animal gets two pages, see? One for my drawing, and one for Tommy's notes."

Cassidy smiles as she flips through the pages. It's weird to see someone who isn't me or Tommy holding the journal. Part of me wants to snatch it back, but I stuff my hands in my pockets so I won't. I trust Cassidy . . . as long as she doesn't trip and drop the journal in the hippopotamus pool.

"I *love* this," she says. Maybe I'm imagining things, but I swear her eyes are a little misty. She hands the journal gently back to Tommy. "You know, I wish I'd had friends like you guys when I was your age."

"Well," I say, "you have friends like us now."

"I don't know," says Cassidy. "Am I cool enough for the two of you?"

"Duh. That's why we let you see the journal."

Cassidy beams. I think she feels very special now.

By the time we get to the back of the park, Tommy has taken photos of every single animal and sneezed about thirty times because I guess he's allergic to Emerald Springs State Park. Also, all three of us are drenched in sweat.

"Dad says there's an eighteen percent chance of heat-stroke today if we spend more than an hour in the direct sun," Tommy pants. "We should monitor ourselves for symptoms. Nausea, difficulty breathing—"

"I feel great," I say, even though my skin is on fire and I'm pretty sure I *am* having difficulty breathing. "It's awesome how Florida is so sunny. It'd probably be sad to live somewhere less sunny. Like, somewhere up north. Wouldn't it?"

Tommy sniffs. Cassidy quirks an eyebrow at me. I shrug. "I was just making an observation," I mumble.

We find Billy at the manatee rehabilitation center, sitting by the edge of the bigger pool and writing notes on a clipboard. He's dressed head to toe in khaki again. Maybe all his clothes are khaki. That'd be weird.

"Peter!" he says, clapping me on the back. I'm not expecting it, so I almost fall over.

Then he and Cassidy both go for a hug at the same time. It's less awkward than last time. I think they're making progress.

"Billy, this is Tommy," I say. "Tommy, Billy."

"Hey there," Billy says. "Are you a manatee fan, too?"

Tommy stares down at his tennis shoes. He can get really nervous around new people. I nudge him with my shoulder and say, "Tommy knows a ton about animals. What was that word you were teaching me the other day, Tommy? *Bio-something?*"

"*Bioluminescence,*" says Tommy, lifting his chin. "It's when an animal produces light from its own body. That's how fireflies glow! Lots of sea creatures are bioluminescent, too."

"You know your stuff!" says Billy.

Tommy smiles shyly.

"Zoe's over here," I say. "Come on!"

I run toward the isolation pool, but Tommy hangs back. I don't want to embarrass him in front of Billy and Cassidy, so I walk back and whisper in his ear, "There *definitely* aren't any rip currents in the manatee pools, Fox."

He gulps and nods. When he approaches the edge of

the pool with me, Zoe surfaces in front of us and exhales right in his face.

"Smells like cabbage," he says, crinkling his nose. Still, he looks happy. Sometimes I think Tommy is more comfortable around animals than people. I can definitely understand that.

"Her cut looks a little better," I say. "I think it's healing."

"It looks like she's swimming around more, too," says Cassidy, coming up behind us with Billy.

"She's doing well," says Billy. "Her appetite has definitely come back with a vengeance!"

"Does that mean we can feed her some lettuce?" I ask.

"She's between feeding times right now, and only staff can feed the manatees, buddy. Sorry."

"Just one head of lettuce?" I say, giving him my most innocent, wide-eyed, please-give-me-what-I-want look.

"Well . . . ," says Billy. He looks at Cassidy. I think they're doing that thing I do with Papa or Tommy sometimes, communicating in their own secret language of expressions and nods and shrugs.

"Okay, Peter," he says. "You got it. But just one."

So Tommy and I get to feed Zoe a chunk of romaine, which is maybe the greatest thing that has ever happened. We break it into pieces and toss them into the water and watch her hoover them up one by one like a big gray vacuum cleaner. I feel like a very successful caretaker. I imagine her getting stronger with every bite. Then I start laughing, because there's just something so funny about the way she eats.

Once I start laughing, Tommy joins me. Laughter is infectious that way. It makes me wonder if all feelings are infectious—if you can catch someone's sadness or anger or joy. Maybe that's what happens when I'm with Zoe. I'm catching her peacefulness.

Once Zoe is done snacking, I pepper Cassidy and Billy with questions so Tommy and I can finish building our case, like: "Should boaters use propeller guards?" And: "How many manatees would there have to be for them to stop being vulnerable to extinction?" And: "What stores sell polarized sunglasses?"

"You know you don't have to cover *everything*," says Cassidy. "Maria and I will be speaking, too."

"That's an all-star lineup!" says Billy. He turns to me and Tommy. "Maria Liu is a manatee conservation *legend*. She knows more about manatees than just about anyone, and she's spent her whole career fighting for them."

I decide right then and there that Maria Liu is my hero.

"But wait," says Billy. "Cassidy, don't you hate speaking in front of people?"

"No! I mean, not *really*," says Cassidy, which is definitely a lie. But maybe it's okay if morality is relative.

"Are you sure?" Billy says. "Remember when you had to give that presentation on manatee grazing behavior down in Key West and you threw up in a bucket?"

Cassidy's cheeks burn. "That was just . . ." She looks at me and Tommy. "Heatstroke."

"So what *aren't* you and Maria covering?" I say, because Cassidy could really use a diversion right about now.

"If you really want to build a case," says Billy, "you can't just talk about *what* people should do. You have to talk about *why* they should do it."

"What do you mean?"

Billy nods toward Zoe. "Why should boaters care about manatees?"

It seems like such a silly question, I don't even know where to start. "Because they should! Because . . . well, because . . ."

"Manatees are a big part of Florida's coastal ecosystem," Tommy chirps.

"And we can't let them go extinct," says Cassidy. "When one species disappears, it has a ripple effect on every other species on the planet. Including us."

"And manatees are just the coolest, aren't they?" says Billy. "I mean, look at her!"

I do look at her, right into her beady eyes. I breathe in and out and let the stillness wash over me. Then I get this funny feeling, like maybe—just maybe—I can see her soul, and maybe she can see mine, too.

I know that sounds weird. I know you can't really *see* a soul. Tommy would say that *soul* isn't a real scientific concept, anyway.

But science doesn't have *all* the answers. Not yet, at least.

For a little while we stay like that—eye to eye and soul to soul. It's totally quiet. Then, without looking away, I say, "Manatees are living creatures. Just like us. They probably want to be safe, just like we want to be safe. They're beautiful—in a funny way—and gentle. It's not fair that we hurt them. It's not—" I stop talking and bite my lip because I know if I say one more word, I'm going to have the worst allergy attack ever.

"That's your case, buddy," Billy says. "That's your case."

From across the pool, Cassidy gives me a smile. It reminds me of the way Tommy smiled when he was crying in my room last weekend. Not that they're the exact same smile, but they make me feel the same way, like happiness and sadness are all mixed up together into some kind of happy-sad smoothie.

Then Tommy's hand is on my shoulder. Tommy's hand isn't like Billy's, clapping my back. It's like a butterfly landing on me—a butterfly with trembling legs. His fingers are shaking. It's weird but I don't move. I just stand there, with Tommy, and Cassidy, and Billy.

And Zoe. She's floating between all of us, bobbing up

and down in the water, gently moving her fins like she's remembering how to swim. Remembering how to be okay. And even though my heart is still aching, and my eyes are burning, and I'm starting to feel light-headed, which I'm pretty sure is one of the symptoms of heatstroke, I want to freeze time. I want this moment to last forever and ever.

TWENTY

Cassidy drops me off first because my house is on the way to Tommy's, but I don't get out of the car right away. There's somebody talking to Mom at the front door and I can't tell who it is . . . until Mom spots me in the back seat of Cassidy's car with my face pressed against the window glass. She waves, and the somebody turns around, and I see his glowering, sunburnt face.

"Hey, isn't that the guy you pointed at on the news?" says Cassidy.

"Given our past encounters with Mr. Reilly, there's an eighty-seven percent chance that this isn't a good sign," Tommy whispers, slouching low in the back seat so Mr. Reilly can't see him.

"No kidding," I grumble.

I thank Cassidy for taking us to Emerald Springs, then hop out of the car and stomp my way across the yard. What on earth is Mr. Reilly doing at my house again? He can't be here to complain about me because I haven't done a thing to him. Well, not since the video of me pointing at him turned me into a local news superstar.

I'm halfway across the yard when Mom says, "Peter, why don't you go in through the garage? I'll be inside in a minute."

There's a hardness to her voice. It's the same voice she uses when she talks to Dad on the phone and tells him that yes, work is going great, and yes, Papa is fine, and no, we don't need any money beyond child support, thanks anyway.

Mr. Reilly, meanwhile, gives me a squint and a frown. I give him a squint and a frown right back, but I decide this isn't the time for direct confrontation. This is the time for sleuth work.

I walk toward the garage, but as soon as I'm out of sight of Mom and Mr. Reilly, I duck behind the row of bushes that lines the front of our house and sneak toward the front door. There isn't much room between the bushes and the house, so the pointy branches scrape my arms and legs. Every time I want to say "Ow!" I bite my lip instead. I bite my lip a lot.

Finally, I'm close enough to eavesdrop.

"The house on Viera Street should be good to go in a few weeks," Mr. Reilly is saying.

Then Mom: "We'll get a property inspector down there once the repairs are done."

"I can tell you right now, the property value has sky-rocketed. New lights, new paint, new air-conditioning. The works."

"What about the floors?"

I hear the clicking of Mr. Reilly's jaw. "Did we talk about the floors?"

"We did," Mom says. "You said you were going to replace them."

"I'll take care of it. Listen, I've got the best guys on this."

Hold on. Am I hearing this right? Are Mom and Mr. Reilly *working together*?

"Real estate," says Mr. Reilly. "That's the ticket, isn't it? Elaine wanted to put all that lottery money in savings, but I said no, we're flipping houses. Buy 'em, fix 'em, flip 'em."

"Do you know when you'll be ready to list your house?" Mom asks.

Mr. Reilly coughs and a glob of saliva lands a few inches away from me in the bushes, which is SO GROSS. "We'll be out of there and into the new digs as soon as the Saunderses hit the road."

"Oh," Mom says. "I ran into Elaine yesterday, and she said she wasn't sure when you'd be moving. Especially because . . ." Her voice trails off.

Mr. Reilly grunts. "Elaine's confused. She's going to drop this divorce nonsense any day now. I'm telling you, we'll be in the new house before the dust settles behind the Saunderses. There better not be much dust, though. I told them to clean it good."

My head is reeling. Mrs. Reilly is divorcing Mr. Reilly? I think back to what she said a couple weeks ago to me and Tommy. *I'm about to make some changes myself, truth be told.*

"Well, I'm looking forward to working with you," Mom says. It sounds like there's something caught in her throat.

Mr. Reilly laughs. "I bet! I'm your best chance at nabbing Real Estate Agent of the Year again, aren't I?"

The edge in Mom's voice grows edgier. "It's not about the title."

When Mr. Reilly speaks again, his voice is so low that I can only hear it by pinching my nose and shutting my eyes, which helps me tune in to my hearing. "Just keep your kid out of my business, okay? He gives me any more grief and I'm finding another agent."

It takes every bit of my willpower to not jump out of these bushes and give Mr. Reilly a piece of my mind. My whole body is shaking and quivering and humming. I feel like a rocket about to take off.

I keep still and wait for Mom to tell him what's what, though, because I know what Mom is like when she's mad, and it's really something. She's been nice to Mr. Reilly before—she might even be working with him—but this is the last straw, it *has* to be . . .

But she doesn't say anything.

The next thing I know, Mr. Reilly is stalking across our yard, our front door is swinging shut, and I'm left sitting here in the bushes, watching Mr. Reilly's glob of saliva drip down into the mulch.

I can't believe it. I can't believe Mom is selling houses for Mr. Reilly. I can't believe she just let him talk to her that way—talk about *me* that way.

When Mr. Reilly reaches the road, he lifts his head and sniffs the air like a hound dog. "Storm's brewing," he says to no one. It doesn't make any sense. The sky is clear blue, not a cloud in sight.

While he's standing there in the middle of the road, Cassidy comes back around the bend after dropping off Tommy. She slams on her brakes to avoid hitting Mr. Reilly. Her wheels screech so loud I'm surprised they don't catch fire.

"Hey, watch it!" Mr. Reilly barks, slapping the hood of her car, which can't be good. I'm not sure how much more her car can take.

Cassidy leans out of the window. "Oh my god, I'm so sorry! There's no visibility at that turn. I didn't see you until—"

Mr. Reilly waves away her apology, then takes his sweet time crossing the street, as if he owns it. As if he owns everything.

I hate him.

I hate him so much I can barely stand it.

I'm so busy hating him I almost forget that I'm supposed to be inside.

Once Mr. Reilly is out of sight and Cassidy's car has puttered out of the neighborhood, I crawl out of the bushes and dart into the house through the garage, my pulse skipping with anger and confusion and I-don't-know-what-else.

Mom is sorting mail in the kitchen. "There you are," she says. "Did you and Tommy have fun at the park?"

"Guess so," I say, trying to sound casual, but it's hard.

It's hard because I'm not just mad at Mr. Reilly. I'm mad at Mom, too. Really mad. I'm mad at her for not defending me. I'm mad at her for working with Mr. Reilly to sell the stupid houses he's buying and flipping with his stupid lottery money. I'm mad at her for keeping it a secret from me.

But I don't want her to know I was listening to their

conversation. I would get in *so* much trouble. So this nasty, burning, boiling feeling inside me—I can't let it out.

I walk away from Mom before I explode. I find Papa in his recliner working on a design I don't recognize.

"What's that?" I ask.

He wiggles his eyebrows. I imagine they're dancing caterpillars. "Something for Zoe," he says.

That's when I remember what I said to get him to relax the other day when he was trying to open the kitchen window—that we could design something for Zoe. That we could do it together.

"It's an installation for the end of the canal," he says. "It's like a roof, see, or an overhang. It will give her a place to seek shelter if she needs it, but it'll still let the sunlight in."

I look at Papa's sketch first one way, then another. It just looks like a bunch of random lines to me. Actually, now that I think about it, his designs have been pretty hard to read lately.

Still, I'm excited.

"That's a great idea," I say. "And hey, Zoe's cut looked better today! Maybe she'll be back soon."

"Well, then, I'll have to get right on this—this—" He looks at me expectantly.

"Marvelous Manatee Sanctuary?" I suggest.

He nods and writes the name at the top of his sketch

paper. It's official. Then he drops his voice to a whisper. "And when she's back, we'll go down to the canal together, you and me, to install it. Won't we?"

"We will," I whisper back. "I promise." Because right now I don't care if Mom doesn't want Papa leaving the house. Right now I don't really care what Mom thinks at all.

Papa gives me a wink. I give him a grin. Conspiracies are fun.

But I still feel unsettled, so I go to my room to draw, which usually makes me feel better. I draw for hours. Mostly manatees, but also hippopotamuses and whooping cranes and other animals from Emerald Springs State Park. And while I draw, I think.

If I speak at the Indigo River Boating Club meeting, Mr. Reilly will be really mad at me.

If Mr. Reilly gets really mad at me, he might pick a different agent for all the houses he's buying and selling, and Mom might not be Space Coast Real Estate Agent of the Year again.

So . . . maybe I *shouldn't* speak at the meeting.

But I can't stop imagining it. I close my eyes and I'm on a stage, speaking to a huge crowd about why we all have to work together to protect the manatees. I see Mr. Reilly in the audience, realizing that he should've listened to me all along. I see Cassidy and Billy cheering me on. Tommy is there in the front row, still in Florida, the finished Discovery Journal in his lap—and right next to him is Papa. His eyes are clear and his leg isn't shaking. He knows exactly where he is. He knows exactly who I am.

I open my eyes, square my jaw, and give myself a nod. I'm speaking at the Indigo River Boating Club meeting, and there's nothing and no one who can stop me.

TWENTY-ONE

I hate to admit it, but Mr. Reilly was right about one thing: there is a storm brewing.

A Category 2 hurricane named Bernard is moving through the Caribbean, and according to Channel 9 News, it will be a Category 3 by the time it hits Florida later this week. The higher the category, the worse the storm. They go up to Category 5, which is basically a hurricane apocalypse.

On Sunday, while Mom is showing houses, Papa and I eat corn chips and watch the news. Hurricane Bernard is a huge churning swirl of colors on the weather map.

"Uh-oh," says Papa.

"Uh-oh," I agree.

I grab my walkie-talkie from my room. "Fox, are you seeing this?"

"I'm seeing it, Falcon. There's a seventy-three percent chance this is going to be a bad one. Dad says we'll probably have to delay our move till after the storm."

"Oh," I say. "That's, um . . . a bummer?"

Except it's not a bummer. It's actually the best news ever.

During a commercial break, I step out into the backyard. The sky is still clear and bright—the color of the eastern bluebird eggs Tommy and I once found in a nest in his backyard. It's hard to believe a storm is coming. But that's the weird thing about Florida—one second, it's the perfect summer day, and the next, it's storming like the world is ending.

Usually the end of the world is a bad thing, but if it means keeping Tommy here, I'm all for it.

Back inside, I find Papa trying to stand. He can't get the footrest of his recliner down. There are corn chips scattered around his chair.

"Papa, what do you need?"

"My tools," he says. "We've got to prepare the house for the storm."

I think back to last summer when Hurricane Lucy blew through town. Papa wasn't living with us yet, but he came to stay with us during the storm and helped Mom get the house ready. He boarded up the windows with plywood and placed sandbags along the outside of the front and back doors to prevent flooding.

The news comes back on and zooms in on Hurricane Bernard on the weather map. The swirl of colors fills the entire screen. I shiver. I'm not usually afraid of hurricanes—sometimes they're even exciting—but there's something about this one I don't like, even if it's really helping me out with my keep-Tommy-in-Florida-forever plan. Maybe Papa is right. Maybe we *should* start preparing the house.

I push his footrest down and help him up, but before I can fetch his toolbox from the garage, Mom gets home and makes him sit right back down.

"Let's all relax," she says, picking up the corn chips. "The hurricane is days away, and it might not even come here. These storm paths always change."

But Papa doesn't look relaxed. He looks frustrated.

And the storm path *doesn't* change. On Monday and Tuesday, I try to keep Papa from seeing the news—it's *I Love Lucy* and nature documentaries all day—but I check the forecast on my phone and watch Bernard inching closer and closer to the coast. It's getting bigger, too, like it's gobbling up the ocean and swelling as it goes.

Then, on Wednesday morning, the front-page headline in the newspaper reads: LANDFALL EXPECTED FRIDAY IN BREVIN COUNTY. That's *my* county.

"Okay," Mom says. "Time to take this seriously."

She cancels her house showings for the rest of the week and we go into hurricane prep mode. Mom picks up nonperishable groceries and water jugs at the store. She gets canisters of gas for her SUV, too, in case the gas stations shut down. When she gets home, I help her move the lawn chairs inside so they don't fly away or crash into our house when Bernard shows up.

Papa tries to help, but Mom won't have it, even when it's time for the sandbags, a trick Papa taught us in the first place.

"We could let him do *something*," I say while Mom and I unload sandbags from her SUV. Boy, they're *heavy*.

"I don't want him getting worked up," she says.

I lug a sandbag up the driveway. "Well," I say through my teeth, "I think it's too late for that."

It's true. The closer Hurricane Bernard gets to landfall, the more antsy and confused Papa becomes. Without anything else to do, he draws Marvelous Manatee Sanctuary designs nonstop, except now it's a Marvelous Manatee *Storm* Sanctuary, and he wants to build it and install it in the canal before the storm hits. He knows Mom would have a fit if she overheard his plan, so he shows me the designs in secret.

"Zoe needs a place to hide from the hurricane," he whispers.

"Zoe is at Emerald Springs," I tell him, again and again, but he just looks at me with glassy eyes. I don't know what to do. Talking about Zoe is supposed to help him calm down, but right now, nothing is calming him down.

I don't feel very calm myself. There's so much to do—help Mom take care of Papa and get ready for Bernard, prepare my manatee presentation in secret, AND make Tommy realize that he can't move to Michigan and should definitely stay here with me forever. This summer break isn't feeling like much of a break.

But it's okay. I'm good at doing lots of things. It's like juggling, I tell myself. I just have to juggle perfectly and not drop any of the balls. No sweat.

Okay, maybe *some* sweat. Especially when Channel 9 starts forecasting 125-miles-per-hour winds and up to a foot of rain on Friday. That's *way* worse than Hurricane Lucy last year.

On the bright side, though, maybe the streets will flood. Maybe trees will fall down and block the roads. Maybe the Saunderses won't be able to go anywhere for days, or weeks, or years. That means more time with Tommy—more time to figure out how to get him to stay for good.

But then, on Wednesday night, when I'm in my room working on my speech for the Indigo River Boating Club meeting, Tommy's voice crackles through the walkie-talkie.

"Peter?"

Something about the way he says my name—my real name, not Falcon—jabs at my heart. Maybe it's just static, but it sounds like he's crying again.

I grab the walkie-talkie. My hands are shaking. Why are my hands shaking?

"Tommy?" I say.

"Peter, my parents changed their minds. We're leaving before the storm. We're leaving tomorrow."

TWENTY-TWO

On Thursday morning, the sky is mottled gray and the air is wet and heavy with the promise of rain. As I walk to Tommy's house—one bare foot in front of the other, down the road that Tommy and I have walked and run and biked a million times—the world is weirdly silent, like it's holding its breath.

Tommy is leaving today. *Tommy is leaving today.* I keep trying to string the words together in my head, but they sound like gibberish. I don't think my brain is working.

My heart isn't, either. All night, I lay awake in bed, waiting for it to tap-dance or explode, but it didn't. It just felt thick and numb like a chunk of rock.

I round a bend in the road and Tommy's house comes into view. There's a giant moving van parked outside. Still, none of it feels real—not even when I reach the house and Mr. and Mrs. Saunders come out dragging suitcases to load in the trunk of Mrs. Saunders's car.

"Peter!" says Mr. Saunders. "We were getting worried you might not swing by."

"Tommy's waiting for you inside," says Mrs. Saunders gently.

They sad-smile at me, the way Mrs. Reilly did that first week of summer. *It's hard, the way things change.* But their voices sound faraway, like I'm hearing them from under-water. I don't say anything. I just walk slowly inside.

The house is empty and silent and dark. The windows are all boarded up for the hurricane, and the walls are bare. My footsteps echo in the emptiness, and I think about how if I screamed, my scream would echo, too. I think about how if I wanted to hide, I wouldn't be able to, because there's nothing left to hide behind.

Tommy is leaving today. The words still don't make any sense. How could they?

I find him in his room, sitting on the floor and hugging his backpack to his chest and staring at I-don't-know-what. He looks so small.

So does his room. An empty room should feel bigger than a full room, because there's more space. But not Tom-my's. Especially not with his window boarded up—the window that looks out over a hibiscus plant. We studied the leaves of that hibiscus plant under Tommy's micro-scope for my science fair project last year.

"I thought you might not come," he says. His voice sounds faraway, too, and garbled, like it's coming through a dying walkie-talkie.

At least he has a voice. I can't find mine.

I drop to the floor next to Tommy and stare at nothing with him. The ground is cold. Tommy's rug is gone.

"Mom and Dad want to be on the road by ten," he says.

I check my watch. There's only a sliver of space between Earth and ten. A few minutes, max. As I watch the planets travel slowly but surely around the sun, the words pass through my head again: Tommy is leaving today.

He's leaving.

He's leaving.

Suddenly I can string the words together perfectly. I can hear them, see them, taste them. They explode like Fourth of July fireworks in my brain, loud and hot, and now my heart is burning up and all I can do is press my sweaty palms flat against the cold ground and practice my deep breaths, but the walls of Tommy's room are closing in on us and I'm going to run out of air any second now, I know I am.

"You'll let me know what happens with Zoe, won't you?" Tommy says. "And how the Indigo River Boating

Club meeting goes? And . . . well, everything? You will, won't you, Peter?"

Words flood my head—all the things I could say. *No. You're leaving. You're really, actually leaving, and Mr. Reilly is moving into your house, and everything is ruined. So you don't get to know about Zoe. You don't get to know about anything.*

But all I can manage is, "The walkie-talkies won't reach that far." I hear my voice like it's someone else's. Sweat stings my eyes and blurs everything. I can't get enough air no matter how much I inhale.

"But we can talk on the phone," says Tommy. He says it like a question. He's waiting on an answer.

I shake my head. The phone isn't the same and he knows it. Anyone can talk on the phone. Only best friends talk with walkie-talkies.

Besides, can't he see what's happening? Can't he see that the walls are closing in and we're going to die any second now?

"Peter? We *will* talk on the phone, won't we?"

He's crying. I know without having to look at his face. I *can't* look at his face. I can't talk, either. I keep my palms pressed to the ground and think about how I should never have agreed to talk to Tommy when he came to my house a couple weeks ago. I should have kept pretending he didn't exist, because then I wouldn't be sitting here right now, feeling the way I feel.

"The poster's in"—hiccup—"there," Tommy says, pointing to his closet. His almost completely empty closet. The poster is the only thing left inside. It looks small and stupid.

"And this is for you," Tommy says, pulling something out of his backpack. "I thought—well, you did all the drawings. So, I thought you'd maybe want to keep it?"

Staring at the journal in his hands—at the yellow cover, at the words *Peter and Tommy's Discovery Journal*—I feel something harden inside me. I curl my hands into tight balls. I clench my jaw so hard it aches. This was supposed to be the summer when we finished the journal. But we didn't. And now we never will. So it's time to stop pretending like it matters.

"I don't want it," I say. The words drop like little stones, cold and hard. "It's a silly journal. We were little kids when we made the Discovery Club, but now . . ." I shake my head. "We should just forget it."

I look Tommy in the eye, daring him to say I'm wrong. He doesn't. He just hugs the journal to his chest and lets the tears and the snot run down his face.

When he speaks again, his voice is so small I can barely hear it. "Peter, don't do this. Please. You know I don't *want* to go. I would do anything to stay."

I stand and grab the poster from the closet. This goodbye stuff is stupid. There's no point in spending time with someone who is just going to leave. If Tommy and I are going to be strangers, we might as well start now. We should've started weeks ago.

I have other things to do, anyway. A *lot* of other things. Like take care of Papa, and get back at Mr. Reilly, and save the manatees. And all the things I need to do, I can do by myself. I don't need anyone's help, especially not someone who's too scared of water—too scared of *everything*—to even get close to a manatee.

"Have fun in Michigan," I say. "Try not to get sucked into any rip currents up there."

I don't look back at Tommy, not even once. I just march right out of the house and down the driveway, past Mr. and Mrs. Saunders and their stupid car and their stupid moving van.

"Peter?" Mrs. Saunders says. "Everything okay?"

"Goodbye, Mr. and Mrs. Saunders," I say.

There. I said goodbye to someone.

It starts to drizzle as I walk home. The rain streaks the colored markers on the poster. By the time I get back to my house, my visual aid is bleeding rainbows, which is just perfect. I run to my room and shove it in my closet before Mom can see it.

It's a good thing, too, because the next thing I know, she's in my doorway.

"How's Tommy?" she says. "How are *you*?"

"Fine," I say. I repeat the word to myself—*fine, fine,*

fine—until it loses meaning.

Mom leans against the doorframe. She's wearing the Mickey Mouse T-shirt she got when we went to Disney World with Papa a few summers back. It was right before Tommy moved into the neighborhood. I remember because I told him all about it the first time we hung out—how Papa had pointed out all the really cool animatronic figures and told me how they worked, and how the water ride had left us all soaked to the bone.

"I know it's really hard to say goodbye," Mom says. "When I was your age, my best friend, Emilie, she moved to—"

"It was easy," I say.

It's quiet for a minute. I fall back on my bed and stare at the ceiling.

"Things have been hard lately, I know," Mom says. "I've been juggling a million and one things. God, we all have, haven't we? And Peter . . . I'm sorry if I haven't been around as much. But if you ever want to talk, you know I'm here. You know that, don't you?"

"What would I want to talk about?"

"Everything? Anything?"

"I'm tired," I say. "I'm going to take a nap."

I feel stupid saying it. I don't take naps—not since I was little, anyway—and Mom knows it. But I need her to leave. Finally, she does.

Her footsteps fade down the hall. I close my eyes and gulp down air. I feel like I just surfaced from the longest dive ever—like two summers ago, when Tommy and I raced underwater at the community pool and I won by staying underwater until my lungs almost burst.

Stupid memories. Stupid everything.

I feel dizzy and thirsty. I go to the kitchen and pour a glass of water, and I gulp down the water like I gulped down the air.

"Can't sleep?" Mom says.

She's sitting at the kitchen table with Papa, working on her laptop while Papa digs through his bucket of screws and nuts and bolts. His hands are shaking. He doesn't look up at me or say anything about Tommy. Doesn't he even care?

Not that *I* care.

A flash of red through the window catches my eye. I move closer and watch a red car move down the street. Mrs. Saunders's red car. Tommy's red car.

It disappears around a turn. I press my forehead to the window glass and stare at the road long after it's gone.

"Peter?" Mom says.

She's behind me now, her hand on my shoulder.

"I was thirsty," I say.

She gives my shoulder a squeeze. "Hey, do you mind

sitting with Papa while I board up the windows? He's really agitated right now."

I nod and take a seat at the table. It's good to have something to do.

While Papa fishes bolts out of the bucket, the sounds of the Weather Channel drift into the kitchen from the living room. "The governor has issued a mandatory evacuation order for certain coastal neighborhoods in Brevin County . . ."

Then Mom starts boarding up the windows and all I hear is hammering.

The noise spooks Papa—a bolt flies out of his hand and he knocks over his glass of water. As I clean up the spill, each bang of the hammer ricochets in my skull. Papa is looking at me, brows furrowed, talking fast. I can't hear what he's saying. "Hold on," I shout, but his lips keep moving.

When there's a break in the hammering, he says, "We're running out of time. We've got to build this manatee storm sanctuary. We just need ten bolts . . . no, *twelve* bolts."

"Zoe's not in the canal, Papa. She's at Emerald Springs. Remember?"

"This design will work," he says, tapping a finger on his latest sketch, which looks even squigglier than his last one. "This is the one. But we need some chicken wire . . ."

The hammer returns, drowning out his voice again. I grab his hand and try to hold it tight, the way he held mine years ago when a wave pulled me under at the beach, but he shakes it off. He keeps rummaging through the junk in the bucket. Screws and bolts clatter as he drops them onto the table and sifts through them like a treasure hunter.

When there's another break in the hammering, he says, "I need to take measurements. I need to go down to the canal."

I tell him Zoe isn't there. I tell him over and over and over again. He looks at me, but he doesn't seem to hear me. Or, if he does hear me, he doesn't believe me. Maybe he doesn't even know me. His shaking hands keep on digging for bolts while Mom boards up window after window. The hazy gray daylight fades behind the wood panels and the house slowly grows dark.

TWENTY-THREE

I wake in the middle of the night drenched in sweat. The monster that was just prowling through my dreams is now screaming outside my window and clawing at the glass.

Except it isn't the middle of the night. My watch says it's eight in the morning, and there's a sliver of murky light coming through the tiny gap between the wood planks that Mom nailed over my window yesterday.

I get up and press an eye to the gap. No monster—just a big, gray, swirling mess. It looks like someone put the whole world in a blender. Rain whips every which way, and leaves and twigs spin through the air like they're caught in tiny tornados. The screaming is the howl of the wind. The clawing is the scratch of tree branches on the window. Hurricane Bernard is officially here.

I reach for my walkie-talkie so I can say "Whoa!" and Tommy can say "Peter, there's a ninety-five percent chance that the majority of lizards in our neighborhood are currently airborne," or whatever weird thing Tommy would say.

Then, with a jolt, I remember Tommy is gone.

Tommy is gone.

Maybe I'm confused. Maybe everything that happened yesterday was one big nightmare. It definitely *feels* like a nightmare.

But when I open my closet, there's my rain-streaked poster for the Indigo River Boating Club meeting. The sight knocks the breath out of me. I'm eight years old again, falling from the monkey bars at recess, landing flat on my back. I feel paper-thin and cold. Because he left. He actually left.

It's not right, waking up in a world where Tommy isn't a walkie-talkie away. All I want to do is go back to sleep. I burrow back under my sheets and shut my eyes tight, but there are monsters lurking at the edge of my dreams. Not just screaming, clawing storm monsters—I can handle those—but moving-van monsters, and Discovery Journal monsters, and science-fair-poster monsters. I *can't* handle those.

Eventually I give up and trudge to the kitchen. I feel like I'm dragging an anvil behind me. There's a stack of just-made waffles on the table, which makes me feel a tiny bit better, but only a tiny bit.

I hear Mom and Papa talking in Papa's room. I don't wait for them. I sit and drown a few waffles in butter and syrup, which is the only thing you can do when the world replaces your best friend with a hurricane.

While I'm eating, Papa shuffles out of his room with Mom right behind him, holding tight to his arm.

"Dad, *please*," she says. "Just sit for a second."

Papa keeps on shuffling, slowly but surely, all the way to the kitchen. He opens cabinets and drawers with shaking hands. "Someone stole the bolts. And the wire. We need the wire."

"I told you, I put all that stuff away," Mom says. "We don't need it. Right now we need to eat breakfast."

She looks at me with bloodshot eyes. She must not have slept well last night. Sometimes I think Mom doesn't sleep well *most* nights. "Peter, do you know what he's going on about? This manatee . . . manatee . . ."

"Marvelous Manatee Storm Sanctuary?" I offer.

"Is this something you were working on together?"

I can hear the accusation. "No," I say. "I mean, not *exactly.*"

A drinking glass shatters at Papa's feet. He's looking for bolts and wire in our cup cabinet. Mom closes her eyes. Her breath is a hiss.

"Papa," I say, "why don't we look at those sketches again? So you can show me how it works."

It takes some convincing, but eventually I get Papa to sit.

"It's anchored in the bank like this," he says, tapping the sketch. "One anchor on each side, see?"

I nod even though the drawing doesn't make any sense. It looks like messy abstract art—not at all the clean, sharp lines Papa used to draw.

"Peter," Mom says, dropping shards of glass into a plastic bin, "what's all this about?"

"He wants to help Zoe," I say.

"And the wire is tented, like a roof . . . ," Papa is saying, his finger still tap-tap-tapping on his sketch pad.

"This manatee business is getting out of hand," Mom says. "First it was Mr. Reilly, and now Papa is all worked up."

I feel a rush of blood to my cheeks. "It's not *my* fault that Papa is—"

"We'll have to drive a couple of stakes down into the canal bed," Papa says. Like he doesn't even hear us. "See?"

I set my fork down. I was the only one eating waffles, and I don't have an appetite anymore. I just don't know how many times I can tell him he's got it wrong. "Papa, Zoe's *not* in the canal right now. And it's already storming, so we *can't* go outside."

Outside, the wind keeps howling. The trees keep scratching. The lights in our house flicker. And even though Papa
is sitting right next to me, it feels like he's looking at me
from across an ocean. A really big, really deep ocean. The
kind of ocean where ships get lost forever and ever. His
whole face crinkles as he frowns. "We shouldn't have let
them take her," he says.

"She's at Emerald Springs to get better," I say.

He shakes his head. "That's what they say. That's what
they want us to think."

I know Papa is just confused right now, but he's also
freaking me out. What if Zoe *isn't* okay? What if she *isn't*
safe at Emerald Springs? How do they protect the animals
there during a hurricane?

And what about Tommy? I don't want to think about
him, but I can't help it. Did he make it out of Florida in
time?

I look at Mom, but her eyes are closed again. She's
back to her deep breathing. She might as well be across an
ocean, too. An even bigger, deeper ocean.

Nobody says anything for a while. Papa draws while
Mom and I breathe and the hurricane roars. Someone
shouts on the TV: "Bernard is proving to be quite the for-
midable opponent, Stacy!"

I peek into the living room. On the TV, a reporter in a
poncho is standing in the middle of the big, gray, swirling

mess, yelling into his microphone as the palm trees behind him bend sideways in the wind. It takes me a second to recognize him as the reporter who interviewed me when Zoe was rescued. I don't know what on earth he's doing outside in the middle of a Category 3 hurricane.

The camera cuts to a road where cars are swerving all over the place like they're go-carts at the state fair. "As you can see, it's madness to be on the roads in these winds, Stacy," the reporter says. "Sheer madness!"

I turn off the TV.

"Peter," Mom says, a little steadier now, "can you sit with Papa while I look for some candles and matches? Looks like we might lose power."

I nod, even though I'm mad at her for basically blaming me for Papa being confused. Even though I think I've been mad at her for a lot of things for a while now.

While she rummages through the kitchen drawers, I think back to Hurricane Lucy last summer. We lit lots of candles and lamps, which made it feel like we were living in a haunted house. Even better, Papa spent hours telling ghost stories, illuminating his face with a flashlight he made himself—the Illustrious Illuminator 3000.

Now Papa is sitting at our kitchen table with shaking hands and wild eyes, drawing lines that never meet.

When Mom disappears down the hall, I grab my phone and dial the number for the Florida Manatee Society. By the fourth dial tone, I realize that nobody will be at the office, because who goes to work during a Category 3 hurricane? Besides Channel 9 reporters.

But then: "Thanks for calling the Florida Manatee Society, central Florida's longest-running manatee research and advocacy center! My name is Cassidy Cawley and—"

"You went to work *today*?"

Papa looks at me, startled.

"Also, hi," I say, a little quieter.

"Hi, Peter," says Cassidy. "No, I'm home. I had the Florida Manatee Society office phone redirected to my cell so I can be on call in case we get manatee injury reports during the storm. I mean, we probably couldn't get the MLC to go out in the middle of this weather . . . but we can make sure the manatees get help as soon as possible when the storm clears! No reports so far, though. Whew."

"Is Zoe okay? Is she safe from the storm?"

Thunder grumbles deep and low. Papa keeps staring at me.

"I was actually just on the phone with Billy," says Cassidy. "Not that we talk all the time or anything . . . Anyway, he said they moved all the manatees at Emerald Springs into an indoor pool. Zoe's probably making friends with the others as we speak! It's her first time swimming with them."

"That's good," I say, giving Papa a thumbs-up. "That's really good."

Another crack of thunder. The lights flicker again. Cassidy says, "Peter, are *you* okay? You sound a little . . . I don't know. Not like yourself."

"I'm fine."

"Okay," says Cassidy. "If you're sure." I can tell she doesn't believe me. I don't believe me, either.

I think about telling her the truth—that my best friend just left, even though I was *sure* I could find a way to get him to stay. That Papa is sick and he's not getting better, no matter how hard I try to be the world's greatest caregiver. That it feels like there's a Category 3—no, a Category 5—hurricane raging inside of me, and everything is spinning out of control.

The next clap of thunder is earsplitting. The whole house trembles. Papa pushes himself back from the table. "Tell Marianne I'm going down to the canal," he says.

I hang up on Cassidy without saying bye. "Papa, what are you *talking* about?" I hear the frustration in my voice. I should practice my deep breaths, but right now I can barely take shallow breaths. "Zoe isn't in the canal," I say for the millionth time. "And even if she was, we couldn't do anything. This thing"—I point at his Marvelous Manatee Storm Sanctuary design—"it doesn't exist. The design doesn't even make sense!"

"Twelve bolts," he murmurs. "No, ten bolts."

I feel my blood starting to boil and I hate it. I don't want to get mad at Papa. But why won't he listen to me? Why can't he just understand?

"Peter?" Mom calls from down the hall. "Can you come here?"

"Hang on!" I yell. "Papa, can you stay here for just a minute? I'll be right back."

He tries to pick up a pile of bolts, but his hands are shaking too bad. The bolts clatter back to the table. My eyes sting.

Maybe I'm not mad at Papa. Maybe I'm mad at myself. Because I'm failing at this caretaking thing, just like I failed at keeping Tommy here.

"Peter?" Mom calls again.

"HANG ON!"

The wind screams outside as I follow Mom's voice to my room, knuckling my eyes all the way. I find her standing in front of my open closet, holding a bag of candles in one hand and my visual aid for the Indigo River Boating Club meeting in the other.

"Peter, what is this?"

"Why are you in my room?"

"I knew there were candles in your closet."

"But it's *my* room. You can't just go snooping around my room without my permission."

Mom sighs. "Peter, stop diverting. What's going on? What's this poster for?"

It's hard to think straight with Hurricane Bernard beating against my window. It's hard to come up with a good lie.

"It's a school project," I say.

Mom's eyes narrow. "A school project over the summer?"

"It's for science class. It was a take-home project."

Mom looks at the poster—at the block letters and the manatee drawings. I drew a blazing Florida sun in the upper right corner and little speedboats along the bottom. It was only last week, but it feels like ages ago now.

"You're about to start middle school," she says. "Why would your elementary school give you a take-home summer project?"

"It's optional," I say, thinking fast. "We aren't going to be graded, it's just—"

"Peter," she says, shaking her head, "you're lying."

Before I can tell her that I'm totally *not* lying, which I guess would be another lie, the power cuts off with a soft *pop*. My room goes dark. At the same time, the wind dies down, and the branches stop scratching the glass, and everything is quiet—quiet enough that I can hear my pulse drumming in my ears. Quiet enough that I can hear Mom's long exhales.

It's not a peaceful quiet—not like how I feel when I'm with Zoe. No, this is the kind of quiet where you hold your breath and wait for something to snap.

"I'm giving a speech at the Indigo River Boating Club

meeting at the end of the month," I say, because suddenly I don't care if my secret plan stays a secret anymore. I don't care, because the storm that was brewing has brewed, and Tommy is gone, and Papa is getting more confused every day. Helping the manatees might be the one thing I can still do right, and I'm doing it with or without Mom's support. "I'm going to help the Florida Manatee Society talk to the boaters about how to not hurt manatees. That's my visual aid. It's what I'll point to."

As my eyes adjust to the dark, Mom slowly comes back into focus. The worry lines around her eyes crease. I wonder how many I've caused.

"Listen," she says. "I know you really care about animals, and I love that about you. But Peter, you *can't* go to that boating club meeting."

Outside, the wind is building up from a sigh to a hum to a roar, and the trees are knocking on my window again like they're begging to come inside. The storm inside me is growing louder, too—lightning shoots through my veins and winds surge in my brain and my voice crackles as I say, "Why not?"

"All of this manatee stuff, it's confusing Papa. And you're too young to be getting involved with—"

"I'm NOT too young!" Each word is a clap of thunder. I've yelled before but never like this. I can't let the storm drown me out—this is too important. It might just be the most important thing ever. "I'm *not* too young," I repeat. "And Papa *likes* hearing about Zoe. It helps him. I've been trying so hard to help him."

"Alright, Peter, let's just take a breath—"

"I'm not taking any stupid breaths! You pretend that taking deep breaths makes you calm, but it doesn't. You're never calm. And why don't you say the real reason you don't want me to go to the meeting? You're afraid of Mr. Reilly because you're working with him to sell all the houses he's buying. But I'm not. I've *never* been afraid of him."

I know by the way Mom's eyes flash in the dark that the storm is inside her now, too. She stands straight and tall like a lightning rod. "I'm *not* afraid of Mr. Reilly. I'm afraid of not being able to support this family. All I asked was that you stay out of his way. God, that's *all* I asked, Peter."

"That's *not* all you asked! You asked me to take care of Papa all summer, even though this was the summer Tommy and I were supposed to finish the Discovery Journal. Other kids aren't taking care of their grandparents who have dementia. They're going to the beach, or playing games, or—" I stop and press my hands against my eyes. I hate what I'm saying. I hope I don't mean it. I love Papa. I wanted to help him. I *want* to help him.

I wait for Mom to tell me off, but when I drop my hands, I see the anger draining out of her face. "I worry every day that I've put too much on you," she says quietly.

"I just thought . . . You and I, we've always made it work, haven't we? Ever since your dad left, we've been a team. And you've always been so close to Papa, so I thought . . . Well, I thought that this could work."

I know what I'm about to say is going to hurt her. But she told me to stop lying, didn't she? So I give her the truth. "We haven't felt like a team for a long time."

Mom's body wilts. "Peter, what do you mean?"

I gesture at the space between us, searching for the right words. "It's like an ocean sometimes."

"Hold on," she yells over the storm, stepping toward me. "I can't hear you."

"I said it's like an ocean—"

I stop. I can barely hear myself. Hurricane Bernard is louder than ever, and suddenly it doesn't sound like it's just coming from outside the house. It sounds like it's coming from *inside*, too. Which doesn't make any sense. How can the storm be in the house?

Mom and I run to my window, but it's still boarded up. I can see the unbroken glass in the crack between the planks.

For a few seconds, we stand there, frozen. Then I bolt out of my room with Mom on my heels.

"Dad?" she calls. "DAD?"

As we race down the hall, a gust of wind pushes against us. Framed photos clatter off a shelf and narrowly miss my head as they fall.

"Watch out!" I holler back to Mom.

In the living room, the world has turned upside down. Magazines and pieces of mail whirl overhead, flapping like birds, along with leaves and twigs and plastic bags. A houseplant teeters and falls—CRASH!—sending a spray of dirt into the air. The fruit basket flies off the kitchen counter and slams into the wall next to the TV. Sideways rain lashes our furniture, beating like a million drums on the couch and Papa's recliner.

I'm the first one to make it to the open front door. It's swinging wildly in the wind, banging against the outside wall.

Out there in the front yard, standing in the middle of the big, gray, swirling mess with his toolbox, is Papa.

I don't think. I just dash out into the storm, hopping over the sandbags and fighting against a wall of wind and rain.

"Peter, STOP!" Mom screams.

But I don't stop, because Papa is out here, and the wind is surging, and he's losing his balance and starting to fall . . .

And that's when time goes all wonky.

TWENTY-FOUR

Time never actually speeds up or slows down, but sometimes it *feels* like it speeds up or slows down. Tommy once told me that what's going on in our brains and our bodies can change how we perceive time.

Like, when Tommy and I were running away from that alligator we found in the marshes by the river, everything happened so fast. One second there wasn't an alligator and the next second there was, and then we were running as quick as we could, and it felt like the whole world was on fast-forward. Later, Tommy said that we were feeling lots of adrenaline.

Sometimes when I'm at school, it's the opposite, especially when the weather is nice and I'd rather be outside making discoveries. I stare at my solar system watch, and

Jupiter seems to move so slowly, like each minute is a year.

But this moment, right now, running toward Papa in the middle of a Category 3 hurricane—this is the first moment in my life where time is speeding up *and* slowing down, which seems impossible. You can't hit pause and fast-forward at the same time, can you?

But it's true. Papa is falling so slowly that it looks like he's dancing underwater. I see his white shirt rippling in the wind. I see every single leaf swirling around him. I see it like Papa is in a snow globe and someone just gave it a shake, and I know I'm going to stop his fall, because all I have to do is get there before the snow settles. I have all the time in the world. I have an eternity.

But I don't make it, because it's all over in a second.

No, less than a second. A millisecond. Half of a blink of an eye.

He's standing in our yard and then he's hitting the ground, just like that.

The wind is shrieking like a chorus of banshees and Mom is screaming and I'm still running toward Papa— I'm still running, but something is hitting the side of my head, and now I'm screaming, too, because it hurts. It hurts so bad, until it doesn't anymore, until the world goes quiet and all I see are gray swirls and then just gray and then just nothing at all.

TWENTY-FIVE

In the back seat of Mom's SUV, I press my forehead against the window glass and watch the spray churned up by our tires. We're slip-sliding toward the hospital down familiar roads, but I barely recognize them tonight. Our town is a stranger, flooded and dark. I give Papa's hand a squeeze. He's sitting beside me, eyes winced shut. He barely squeezes back.

"Peter," Mom says, too loud, "what day is it?"

"You asked me that five minutes ago. And don't yell. You're hurting my head."

"I'm not yelling," she yells. "What day is it?"

Mom is worried I have a concussion, which is something that can happen when you have a head injury. An example of a head injury is Hurricane Bernard clobbering

173

you on the side of the head with a ginormous airborne tree branch. That's what happened to me, at least. Ever since, Mom has been checking me for amnesia.

"It's Saturday morning," I say. "Three thirteen a.m."

"And do you remember everything that's happened since you woke up?"

"Yes," I say, but I replay it all in my head just to make sure.

One second that branch was clobbering me, and the next thing I knew, I was lying on the couch with an ice pack on my head and the worst headache in the world. I had no idea what was going on. I didn't know why Papa was crumpled on the floor by the front door, or why Mom was crying and cursing and trying to lift him. I didn't know why our house was such a mess, either.

When I sat up, Mom ran over and pulled me into the tightest hug ever. She cried into my hair. She held my face between her palms and kissed my forehead over and over again.

It took a few minutes for me to remember everything, and for Mom to explain what I'd missed. How she'd barely managed to get me and Papa inside after we ran out into the storm. How Papa had collapsed again by the door and couldn't stand. How she'd called 911, but the emergency room couldn't send out an ambulance in the middle of a hurricane. "I think he broke his hip," she said. "I think he really broke it this time."

Even though I felt like someone was smashing my head over and over again with a mallet and standing up made me dizzy, I helped Mom lift Papa onto the couch. It was hard and we were scared of hurting him, but we couldn't just leave him on the floor like that.

Then we waited out the storm. I iced my head and listened to storm updates on a battery-powered emergency radio I found in Papa's toolbox. Mom paced and called 911 every hour and swore every time they said they couldn't send an ambulance out yet. Papa sat on the couch, twisted in pain, refusing to eat or drink or take his pills.

Finally, in the middle of the night, the wind stopped roaring and the rain stopped hissing and everything went spookily quiet. Mom called 911 again, but this time they said they didn't have any emergency vehicles to spare. They said it would take several hours to get to us. Mom told them it had already *been* several hours. She also said some other things I can't repeat.

Then she hung up and announced, "The SUV is all-terrain."

And that's how we ended up slip-sliding toward the hospital at three a.m.

It's madness to be on the roads in these winds. Sheer madness! That's what the Channel 9 reporter said yesterday. Well, Hurricane Bernard might be mostly gone now, but it's definitely still madness to be on the roads.

Most of them are flooded, for one thing. Mom's SUV is supposed to work in all terrains, but I guess not just-after-a-hurricane terrain because the tires keep losing traction and we're drifting all over the place like it's bumper cars, except a lot scarier. It's a good thing there are hardly any other cars on the roads.

Also, some streets are blocked by trees or poles that Bernard knocked over, so we have to keep turning around and finding another way to the hospital.

"Shoot!" Mom says when we hit another dead end, except it isn't really *shoot*. She tries to make a U-turn and the car drifts into a guardrail with a crunch. It takes her a few seconds and a few more *shoot*s to get us going again.

It's quiet for a few minutes. My eyes drift shut. I'm so tired. I don't think I've ever been this tired in my whole entire life.

Then Mom says, "Peter, keep your eyes open! You can't fall asleep if you have a concussion."

"I know," I say, because she's told me fifty times already. "I was just squinting."

She's watching me in the rearview like a hawk, so I stretch my eyes open as wide as they'll go, which is hard, because it feels like there are tiny anvils weighing my eyelids down.

"If you get sleepy, remember to pinch your leg. Okay,

Peter? Pinch your leg!"

While I sigh and pinch my leg, Papa starts mumbling something about not wanting Marianne to know that he's hurt. I don't think he realizes Marianne is the one driving. His eyes are still squeezed shut.

"What's he saying?" Mom asks.

I wince. "You're yelling again."

"We can't worry Susan, either," Papa says. Susan is Nana, who died when I was three. "Tell her I'm fine," he says, but we can't and he's not.

I give his hand another squeeze because I don't know what else to do. I wish I was strong enough to pull him out of the pain. I wish I was strong enough to pull him out of the fog in his mind, too. But I'm not. Maybe I never was.

I press my throbbing head to the window again. All of Stonecrest must have lost power. Houses stare back at me with dark windows for eyes. Trash swirls on roads-turned-into-rivers and dead traffic lights dangle on wires.

It feels like the world just ended.

It feels like sheer madness.

TWENTY-SIX

After my CT scan, a.k.a. my cranial computerized tomography scan, the nurse gives me a lollipop, which makes me feel like a little kid, but it's orange so I eat it. Orange is the best ice pop flavor, so I figure it's the best lollipop flavor, too.

Also, it's a nice distraction from how much my head and butt hurt.

My head hurts for the obvious reasons. The nurse gave me painkillers, but it still feels like someone is drumming my skull. I don't have a concussion, though, so that's good.

My butt hurts because these hospital waiting room chairs are the *worst*. They look soft until you sit in them and realize the cushion is a lie.

I've sat in these chairs with my butt hurting once before,

when Mr. Saunders broke his arm falling out of a tree. I went with Tommy and his parents to the hospital so Mr. Saunders could get a cast and decide—a.k.a. swear to Mrs. Saunders—that he'd never play paintball again. That's how Tommy and I got our industrial-strength walkie-talkies.

The hospital was a lot busier that day, and the lights were brighter. Now the hospital is running on backup power because of the hurricane. The lights are low, and the vending machines and TVs aren't working.

I stare at the not-working vending machines. They look so gloomy and sad.

"Are you hungry?" Mom says. She's gone from chewing her nails to clicking them on the wooden armrest between us. "They have snacks in the gift shop. I think I saw chips. You like chips."

"I'm okay," I say.

She shifts in her seat. Maybe her butt hurts, too. "You should take a nap. You've been up all night. Don't mind me. Just get some rest, okay?"

"I'm not tired," I say, which isn't true. It's 5:04 a.m. according to the planetary alignment of Jupiter and Earth, and that means I haven't slept in almost twenty-four hours.

But ever since the nurse wheeled Papa away for X-rays, Mom hasn't been able to sit still, which makes it hard to relax. Also, every time I close my eyes, I'm running out into the hurricane again and watching Papa fall too slow and too fast.

So I stare at the sad vending machines while the pain-killers kick in. The drumming in my head gets quieter. The world gets fuzzier. It's hard to think, which is fine by me. Sometimes thinking is the worst.

Eventually, a woman in a white coat finds us in the waiting room. She has dark hair spilling out of a messy bun and a kind face. Her name tag says Dr. Agrawal.

Mom and I stand. Mom's hand grips my shoulder like a talon.

"We gave him some painkillers and he's resting now," Dr. Agrawal says. She pauses. It's not a good pause. "But I'm afraid he's broken his hip. He needs surgery."

I see Mom place her hand over her heart. I see her lips moving, and the doctor responding, back and forth, but I can't hear what they're saying. I just hear *broken* and *surgery*, echoing in my brain over and over again like they're the only two words in the universe.

Then I hear Dr. Agrawal say, "And you don't know why he went outside in the middle of a hurricane?"

Mom glances at me. It's fast, but I catch it. I *feel* it.

"I don't," she says. "I keep the front door locked and dead-bolted, I swear I do, but—"

"I wasn't suggesting anyone is to blame," Dr. Agrawal says gently. "I did want to ask, though. He seemed a little confused when we took the X-rays. Does he have . . . ?"

"Alzheimer's," Mom says.

The doctor nods. "My mother has Alzheimer's. It's the hardest thing, isn't it?"

Mom is quiet. Now she's the one staring at the sad vending machines.

Then she says, "What happens now?"

"The surgeon will be in as soon as the roads clear. Until then, your dad can rest. Those painkillers are probably kicking in as we speak."

Maybe they gave him the same painkillers they gave me. Maybe his world is getting fuzzy, too. Although I think his world has been fuzzy for a while now.

"Can I see him?" I ask.

"Peter, I should get you home," Mom says.

"You two shouldn't go anywhere with the roads in these conditions," Dr. Agrawal says. "It's a miracle you made it here safely. This is a little unconventional, but we can set you up with a room here so you don't have to sleep in the waiting room." She leans in toward me. "Those seats are pretty uncomfortable, huh?"

"The worst," I say.

She gives me a smile. If I was capable of smiling right now, I'd return it.

The doctor leads us down the hall to Papa's room. The bed closest to the door is empty. Papa is in the farther bed by the window. His eyes are closed, and his chest is rising and falling slowly. I wonder what he's dreaming about. I wonder if he's still in pain.

"It's good that he's sleeping," Dr. Agrawal whispers.

Mom holds Papa's hand for a minute. Then she says, "Let's go, Peter." But she doesn't seem to want to leave yet. So we don't. We stand side by side, watching Papa breathe, even after Dr. Agrawal steps out of the room.

It's raining again. Not angry hurricane rain—soft, lonely rain, trickling down the window glass. I don't know how long I stand there, watching the rain, but eventually Mom says, "He wanted to go to engineering school. Did I ever tell you that?"

I look at her—at the hair matted to her face and the bags under her eyes. She crosses her arms over her chest like she's hugging herself.

"Papa?" I say.

She nods. "When he was young. But he couldn't afford it. So he started working in his dad's watch shop and never stopped. But he made sure that I could go to college. He saved up. And when your dad left, he was there, every step of the way. He did everything for me, Peter. That's why I had to try to do everything for him. And now . . ."

And now.

I listen to the rain and try to hold on to the fuzziness

in my head because I know something awful is waiting on the other side.

I wasn't suggesting anyone is to blame, Dr. Agrawal said.

But there is someone to blame, and Mom and I both know it.

When we step into the hall, the nurse who gave me the orange lollipop is waiting for us. He leads us to an empty room a few doors down.

"We don't usually do this," he says. "But make yourselves comfortable."

I lie down on the bed by the window and think about how this is my first time spending the night in a hospital. Except, it's not really night anymore. The sun is starting to rise. I watch it through the rain.

Mom sits on the edge of my bed and ruffles my hair, the way she used to when I was little. "Try to get some sleep," she says. And suddenly I remember what I told her before Papa went out into the storm. *We haven't felt like a team for a long time.*

I curl into myself and shut my eyes against the rising sun. Colors dance on the inside of my eyelids. I watch them until they start taking shape—until they begin to swim through canals, past Mr. Reilly's house, past a blinking neon sign that says "Country Music Capital of the World," into a cove ringed with palm trees where Papa sits in his canoe with his red toolbox and a bucket full of bolts and gears.

Except it's not Papa, it's me, and the sky isn't blue, it's a big, gray, swirling mess, because the hurricane is back. And those aren't birds—they're pages of the Discovery Journal, flapping in the wind. I stand on my tiptoes and try to catch them, but the canoe rocks and I'm losing my balance, falling into the water, holding my breath.

I spin and spin in the dark river, not sure which way is up, waiting for Papa's hand to find mine. I wait until my head hurts and my lungs ache. He never comes.

That's when I see Zoe. I'm going to run out of air any second now, I know I am, but I swim toward her. I swim like mad, arms and legs pumping, lungs screaming.

I'm nearly there—I can almost touch her—but then, just as I reach out my hand, she dissolves into a hundred thousand minnows that dart through my fingers and disappear.

TWENTY-SEVEN

Breakfast is a granola bar and gummy bears from the hospital gift shop. Except it's not really breakfast, because I went to sleep at dawn and woke up at noon. So it's more like lunch.

I eat in the waiting room and stare at strangers. Last night it was just me and Mom here. Today there are a few others—a couple doing a crossword puzzle together, an old woman rummaging through her purse. She can't seem to find what she's looking for.

The power is back on, which means the TV is on, too. Channel 9 shows footage of water gushing down streets and firefighters rescuing a man who was stranded on the roof of his flooded beach house.

"God," Mom says. "Can you imagine?"

She's been pacing the waiting room ever since they took Papa into surgery. She says she got a little sleep this morning. I don't believe it. She says she'll eat breakfast later. I don't believe that, either.

She pulls out her phone and her face tenses. "Six missed calls from your dad. He wants to know if we made it through the storm okay."

It's not funny but I almost laugh. We definitely didn't make it through the storm okay.

"I should call him back," Mom says.

When she steps away, I look for a remote so I can change the channel to something that isn't terrible, but I can't find it. So I ask a woman at the nurse's station if she has spare paper and a pencil. She hands me some flyers advertising an upcoming hospital bingo night. "They're blank on the back," she says.

But when I sit back down, I realize I don't have anything to draw, because all I know is animals and I don't want to draw animals anymore. Especially manatees. I don't even want to *think* about manatees.

I don't want to think about anything.

So I go back to staring at the vending machines, which are lit up now and humming, and I rub the bump on the side of my head. It's a big one.

Mom returns a few minutes later, holding her phone out to me. "He wants to talk to you," she mouths.

I shake my head. I never take Dad's calls. But Mom gives me a look that says, *Come on, Peter,* and I'm too tired to argue right now. I think Mom is, too.

I take the phone. "Hello?"

"Peter," Dad says. It's been a while since I've heard his voice. It's deep and low like a tuba. I wonder if my voice will be like that someday. "Your mom was just catching me up. It sounds, uh . . . It sounds tough over there right now." He pauses. "How are you feeling?"

The question throws me for a loop. Dad has never asked how I'm feeling before. Dad doesn't talk about feelings.

Then I realize he means my head, not my heart.

"Fine," I say, even as the lump on my head throbs.

"Good. That's good." He coughs. "Well, like I was telling your mom, if you need anything . . ."

I want to tell him that we don't need anything from him. We don't *want* anything from him. He left. He doesn't get to call us now and act like Mr. Helpful.

But there's no fight in me, and I don't want to make a scene in front of Mom. "Yeah," I say. "Okay."

There's a long silence. Dad coughs again. Then Dr. Agrawal and a surgeon in green scrubs enter the waiting room and make a beeline for Mom.

"I have to go," I tell Dad.

"Right. Okay. Well, I, uh . . . I love you, Peter."

He chokes on the word *love.* I hang up and join Mom.

"I'm happy to say the operation went well," the surgeon says matter-of-factly, like it's just business and not my entire world. "There were no complications. But he's going to have to stay here for at least a few days so we can keep an eye on him, especially with the dementia."

Mom asks a flurry of questions without giving them time to answer, then apologizes and settles on one: "Will he walk again?"

"I want to say yes, but we don't know yet," Dr. Agrawal says. She doesn't say it like it's just business. She says it like it matters. I decide I like her. "Some patients recover full mobility after a hip replacement. Others . . . Well, at this stage, it's watch and wait."

I might like Dr. Agrawal, but I hate watch and wait. I'm sick of it. Judging by Mom's heavy sigh, she's sick of it, too.

Still, it's good news, isn't it? The operation went well. No complications.

But when they let us check on Papa, he looks so small under his bedsheets that my eyes water. Maybe I'm allergic to hospitals. A tube runs from his arm to a weird-looking machine beside his bed. The machine is beeping. It's the only sound.

Mom sits beside him for a minute while I stand back. When she steps into the bathroom, I take the chair beside Papa's bed.

The machine keeps beeping. Papa's chest rises and falls.

Finally, I say the only thing I can say: "I'm sorry." I bury my face in my hands and say it again and again: "I'm sorry, I'm sorry, I'm sorry."

But I know that however many times I say it, it won't be enough. Because everything that's happening right now is happening because of me.

If I hadn't made that poster for the Indigo River Boating Club meeting, Mom wouldn't have found it in my closet, and we wouldn't have fought about it, and we would never have left Papa alone in the kitchen when he was so confused.

And Papa wouldn't have gone outside in the middle of a Category 3 hurricane to build a Marvelous Manatee Storm Sanctuary if I hadn't filled his head with manatees in the first place.

Mom was right. All this manatee stuff got out of hand.

I thought I could do everything this summer. I thought I could finish the Discovery Journal, and thwart Mr. Reilly, and save the manatees, and take care of Papa, and keep Tommy, and maybe change the world along the way.

But I couldn't do any of it.

I feel so stupid. What was I thinking? I'm just a kid. A kid who gets into too much trouble. A kid who breaks everything he tries to fix.

So maybe I should stop trying to fix anything.

TWENTY-EIGHT

Home feels wrong without Papa.

It's weird, because he's only been living with us for about six months. But I guess it was long enough for me to get used to him being around.

I try watching *I Love Lucy* and eating chocolate mint ice cream and corn chips without him, but it isn't the same. The house feels too quiet. Too empty.

It's worse when Mom is at work or visiting Papa at the hospital without me—when I'm here all alone with nothing to do and nobody to take care of.

I keep staring at my phone, waiting for Tommy to call. But why would Tommy call after everything I said to him? After everything I *didn't* say to him?

It's not much better when Mom is home, though. Since

Papa's fall, she's picked up a new hobby: cleaning.

It started with everything that got messed up when Hurricane Bernard turned our house upside down. The boards had to be taken off the windows, and the patio furniture had to go back outside. There was broken glass to sweep. Leaves and twigs and dirt had blown inside, and a few lizards, too—mostly brown and green anoles, a.k.a. Discoveries #22 and #31.

Once the house looked normal—well, normal minus Papa—Mom dusted and vacuumed and disinfected. She pulled weeds in our front yard and washed the SUV. She even wiped down the leaves of our fake houseplants with a wet paper towel, which I've never, ever seen her do.

"It's spring cleaning," she told me. But it's not spring. It's midsummer.

Before Hurricane Bernard, the summer was flying by. There were a million things to do and not enough time to do them. Now the rest of summer stretches before me like an endless ocean. There are still six weeks left until school starts. What am I supposed to do until then? How am I supposed to fill my time?

One day, a week after the hurricane, I find Mom vacuuming.

"Do you need help?" I yell over the roar.

"No," she yells back. "You just relax! Do something fun!"

She smiles. She's been smiling at me a lot this past week.

I don't get it. Why is she being so nice to me *now*, when · she should be furious with me for what happened to Papa?

Anyway, I can't relax, and nothing feels fun. I don't even want to go outside. It's too hot. There are too many mosquitos. Heat and mosquitos never used to keep me indoors, but I guess they do now.

I decide to clean my room. I rearrange my books so they're in alphabetical order, then rearrange them again so they're grouped by color instead. Afterward, I sort through a stack of report cards and homework from fifth grade and carry a pile to the recycling bin in the garage.

When I get back inside, Mom is on her phone. "He didn't tell you?" she's saying. "My dad—his grandfather—hasn't been feeling well. Peter's been helping me take care of him this summer. . . . I know. He really is." She waves me over.

My stomach flips as I walk toward her. I've been waiting for Tommy to call. I've been wanting to talk to him so bad. But now that I'm *actually* about to talk to him, I have no idea what I'm going to say. And why is he calling Mom instead of me?

I grab Mom's phone and run to my room. "Hello?"

"Hi, Peter!"

It's not Tommy. It's Cassidy.

"I was just talking to your mom. I'm so sorry about your grandfather. God, that must be really hard."

My grip tightens on the phone. "I'm fine."

"Okay . . . Well, hey, I wanted to see if you could come into our office sometime this week. Maria would love to meet you before the Indigo River Boating Club meeting. I could pick you up, if you want?"

I look out my window at the canal. There's a palm tree on the bank that split in two during the hurricane.

"I'm not going to the Indigo River Boating Club meeting," I say.

"Wait, really?" says Cassidy. "Are you sure? You seemed so excited."

"I'm sure."

Silence. Part of me wants to fill it with questions. I want to ask how Zoe is doing, and if she's any closer to being released, and if any manatees were injured during Hurricane Bernard. But I don't.

"Well, if you change your mind—"

"I won't," I say.

I hang up but keep looking out at the canal. I can see part of the Reillys' yellow house from here. I wonder if they're still there or if they've already moved into Tommy's house. I wonder if Mrs. Reilly has divorced Mr. Reilly yet. Then I tell myself to stop wondering because none of it matters. It's not my business. It never was.

I don't realize Mom is standing in my doorway until she says, "Peter?"

I whip around. "How long have you been there?"

"You got another letter from Carter Middle School in the mail," she says, placing an envelope on my desk. "Why aren't you going to the boating club meeting?"

"Um. You told me I *can't* go to the meeting. Remember?"

She sits on the edge of my bed. "I was angry," she says. "And overwhelmed. But I meant it when I said that I love that you love animals, Peter. I really admire that about you."

She squints at me like I'm blurry and she's trying to bring me back into focus. "Maybe speaking at that meeting would be good for you. This Florida Manatee Society, it seems like a great organization. Cassidy seems nice. So, listen, if this is important to you—"

"It's not," I say. "I don't care about the boating club. I don't care about manatees."

Mom stares at me. I stare past her, at the wall. At nothing.

"Hey, Peter? You know what happened to Papa wasn't your fault. If I made you feel like it *was* your fault—I'm so sorry. He just got confused. He got really confused."

Maybe it was better when Mom was an ocean away. Right now, she's so close I can hardly breathe.

Finally, she stands. "If you change your mind about the meeting," she says, "just know that I'll support you. I'll always support you, Peter. Not perfectly, God knows. But I'll do better. I promise."

She taps the envelope on my desk on her way out. When she's gone, I open it and find my sixth-grade class schedule. I got the electives I wanted: art and drama. But it doesn't matter anymore.

I stuff the letter in the bottom of my sock drawer next to the walkie-talkie, then look around my room for more things to clean.

I spot the manatee poster in my closet. I have to fold it in half and jump on it a few times to get it to fit into the recycling bin.

TWENTY-NINE

Papa is transferred from the hospital to Dogwood
Physical Rehabilitation Center on the Fourth of July. Mom
and I don't watch fireworks that night, but we hear them
exploding in the distance.

Papa is only supposed to be at Dogwood for a week, but
the painkillers he's taking have him more confused than
ever. Dexter, the physical therapist teaching Papa to walk
again, tells Mom that progress is "two steps forward, one
step back." So one week turns into two, then three, then
who-knows-how-long.

July crawls along slower than a Florida apple snail,
a.k.a. Discovery #68. Some days, Mom drops me off at
Dogwood before she goes to work. I hang out with Papa

in his room. He mostly sleeps. When he's awake, he rarely recognizes me.

Other days, Mom plans things for the two of us. She takes me shopping for new school clothes, or drives us out to a state park, as if I still cared about making discoveries. I don't know why she suddenly wants to spend so much time together.

One morning she wakes me up super early when it's still dark. "We're going to the beach," she announces brightly.

I'm confused. The two of us haven't gone to the beach together in years. I've gone with Papa, and with Tommy and his parents, but not Mom. Also, it's SO EARLY.

"Can we go later?" I mumble.

Her answer is a firm no.

A few minutes later, we're driving down quiet streets. The world is still sleeping. It reminds me of the drive to the hospital in the middle of the night, but it's not as dark. Streetlights dot the way like stars, and there's the hint of a glow on the horizon. Mom steps on the gas. "We can't miss the sunrise," she says.

We park near the boardwalk and follow a rickety wooden ramp down to the beach. I've never seen it so empty or still before. There are no sun umbrellas, no kids playing in the shallows. Just the ocean. As the sky over the water turns orangey-purple, Mom lays out a blanket on the sand and pulls two thermoses out of a tote bag.

"Coffee," she says.

"I thought I wasn't allowed to have coffee."

Mom shrugs. "There's no point in rules if you never break them."

"Um, are you feeling okay? Because that's not something you would say if you were feeling okay."

"Come on," she says. "Try it."

I take a sip out of one of the thermoses and immediately spit it out. "Ew!"

Mom laughs, but it fades fast. I'm looking out to sea—at the waves I used to try to grab and hold on to when I was little—but I can feel her looking at me. "Do you want to go for a swim?"

"No," I say, even though I used to love swimming in the ocean. Even though this is my first time going to the beach this summer. Maybe my only time.

We watch the sun rise in silence. Orange and purple turn to yellow and the first hint of blue. It's pretty but sad, too. All I can think is that I wish Tommy was here.

I never knew that missing somebody could literally hurt. Every time I think about him—basically every other second, because it turns out I'm pretty terrible at not-thinking—I feel a sting right in the center of my chest, like a bee somehow found my heart.

He still hasn't called. But why would he? He's probably

having an amazing time in Michigan. He probably has a new best friend who never snaps at him or says horrible things.

Kind of like how Papa now has a whole team of caretakers who never get frustrated with him or embarrassed by him.

Even Zoe has people like Billy who can take care of her in ways that I couldn't.

"Peter?" Mom says. She's squinting at me in the glare of the sun. The wind tosses her hair. "I need you to be okay."

I hug my legs to my chest. With my chin on my knee, I watch a huge wave build on the horizon. It crashes onto the shore, and the foamy tide almost reaches our blanket. I scoot back, away from the water's edge.

THIRTY

"What's the verdict?" Dexter asks.

From my chair in the corner of the exercise room at Dogwood Physical Rehabilitation Center, I hold up a sheet of paper with a big number 10 drawn on it.

Dexter pats Papa lightly on the shoulder. "Look at that! You're at the top of your game today."

Dexter, who is big and muscly and looks like a physical therapist in a Hollywood movie instead of a physical therapist in real life, believes that encouragement is a key part of the recovery process. It was his idea for me to hold up high scores whenever Papa does something impressive, like stand without his walker or take a step without holding on to Dexter's arm.

Papa blinks at me. "Thanks, Paul."

My stomach squirms the way it always does when Papa forgets who I am, but I don't tell him my name is Peter. According to Dexter, correcting Papa isn't very encouraging. I just smile. Or, at least, I twist my mouth into what feels like a smile. It kind of hurts.

"Alright, let's see two more steps," says Dexter. "You've got this."

I like Dexter. Still, it's hard to watch someone else take care of Papa.

I look around the exercise room. There are always a few other patients and therapists here. Today a woman in a cardigan is lifting tiny purple dumbbells in a corner of the room. Nearby, old Mr. Harrington—Papa's latest roommate at Dogwood—is sitting on a big blue exercise ball, telling his therapist that he "doesn't need any dang help."

Everyone here is hurt somehow, but their injuries are all physical. None of them are confused like Papa.

Dexter says Papa has "good" days and "better" days. So far, today is a "better" day. Papa can move around a bit, and he isn't trying to escape the building or asking the staff to fetch his tools. I think he's just happy I brought him some chocolate mint ice cream.

After physical therapy, he refuses to eat anything but the ice cream for lunch, which is probably for the best, because Mr. Harrington's plate of quivering cafeteria lasagna doesn't look so good.

I sit with Papa and Mr. Harrington in their room while they eat. The rooms at Dogwood are cheerier than at the hospital, at least—there are pictures of beaches and fish on the walls and a plant in the corner. The TV is bigger, too. Mr. Harrington is watching a tennis match, giggling every time the players grunt when they hit the ball. I've never watched tennis before, but I like watching the ball sail back and forth and back and forth. It's kind of hypnotizing.

"I've got it!" Mr. Harrington blurts, making me jump. "I knew you looked familiar—it's been itching at my brain for days now. You're that manatee boy!"

Papa looks from me to Mr. Harrington. His bushy eyebrows twitch. "Zoe," he says. Well, at least he remembers *her* name.

"That's what you called her, isn't it?" Mr. Harrington says. "Zoe." He laughs a raspy laugh. "I saw you on the local news. It sure was funny, you calling out that neighbor of yours. Boy, you looked *mad.*"

Suddenly Papa grips the handrails on his bed. "I need to get down to the canal," he says, his voice dry enough to start a fire. "I have to install the—the—" He shakes his head, unsettling his wispy white hair. "I have to install it before the storm hits."

I think about what Dexter says—correcting Papa isn't very encouraging. I think about how every time I've corrected him before, it never really helped. So I just grab his hand and wait for the storm inside of him to pass.

"I need my tools," he whispers, pulling me close. "I think somebody hid them."

Across the room, Mr. Harrington keeps eating his lunch like nothing is happening. He's only been at Dogwood for a few days—he's Papa's fourth roommate—but I guess he's already gotten used to Papa's confusion. Also, he seems really into the quivering lasagna.

"We have to be careful," Papa continues. "They don't want us to leave. Just follow me, okay?"

He tries to stand, but his face crinkles in pain and he falls back onto the bed, breathing hard. I grip his hand tighter. Maybe today isn't really a "better" day. Maybe it's just a "good" day, which really means a terrible day.

I sit beside him until the storm passes and he quiets down. The painkillers have him feeling super tired. When Mom comes to pick me up later in the afternoon, he's snoring softly. His face looks peaceful. Maybe he's not so confused in his dreams.

"How is he today?" Mom whispers.

"He's good," I say.

Mr. Harrington glances at me from across the room. He likes to say he can't hear very well, but I don't know about that. He *does* have a lot of ear hair, though.

I try again: "I mean, he's about the same."

Mom pats down Papa's hair and gives him a kiss on the cheek. Usually she sits with him for a while before we leave, but today she doesn't even set her briefcase down.

"Let's get going," she says. "It's almost dinnertime."

I'm not sure what she means by "dinnertime." We eat at different times every night, especially since Papa has been in rehab.

She's chatty on the drive home. "Today is going to be a good day," she says. "Can you feel it?"

I give her my you're-being-suspicious look. "Not really," I say. "Also, the day is more than halfway over."

Mom just smiles.

When we get home, she dices vegetables for a stir-fry and puts me to work mincing garlic with the mincer she ordered from a TV infomercial last week. She's been ordering a lot of infomercial products since Papa's surgery. I'm on my fourth clove when the doorbell rings.

"Peter, can you get that?" Mom says. There's something funny about her voice.

I set down the mincer and walk to the door, imagining another hurricane outside, just waiting to clobber me on the head again.

Then I wonder if it's Mr. Reilly. Usually I'd be ready to tell him off, but right now I don't think I have it in me, and that scares me. Being ready to tell off Mr. Reilly was my deepest truth. Who am I without my deepest truth?

I open the door just a smidge, just enough to peek out.

It's not a hurricane.

It's not Mr. Reilly, either.

It's a skinny boy with glasses and dark curly hair and a *Science Daily* T-shirt, carrying a giant backpack and squinting in the sunlight.

THIRTY-ONE

"What're you doing here, Tommy?" I hiss through the barely open door. I can't let Mom know that he's here, because maybe he ran away from home and I need to hide him. Or maybe he's on the run from the police!

Aw, who am I kidding? Tommy would never break the law.

"I'm visiting you," he says.

"But how did you *get* here?"

"I flew." He scrunches his face, then sneezes. I didn't know how much I missed the sound of his sneeze till right now. "Did you know that the oxygen in a plane's emergency oxygen masks only lasts for about fifteen minutes?"

I shake my head.

"We didn't have any emergencies, luckily," he says. "Just some turbulence."

"But . . . Michigan."

He nods. "That's where I boarded the plane."

Tommy and I stare at each other.

I know he's here—I mean, *obviously* he's here, he's standing right in front of me—but it doesn't seem real. I'm scared that if I look away, even for a second, he might disappear. So I look at him really, really hard. I don't even blink.

"Um," he says. "Can I come in? It's hot. Also, a mosquito just bit me and there's at least a four percent chance it was carrying a deadly virus."

Before I open the door any wider, I check to make sure Mom is still busy in the kitchen in case I really *do* need to hide Tommy. I almost scream when I see her leaning against the back of the couch, watching us with a smirk. "Peter, are you planning on keeping our guest outside all evening?"

That's when I realize a conspiracy is afoot.

I open the door all the way, and Mom pretends to gasp. "Tommy, what a surprise!"

It's not very convincing, but Tommy looks alarmed. "Really? My dad talked to you on the phone yesterday to confirm my flight information."

Mom laughs. "Oh, well, I guess the jig is up. I was

talking to Tommy's parents last week, Peter, and we thought it might be fun if Tommy came to visit for a little while before summer ends."

I look from Mom to Tommy. "You flew here from Michigan by yourself?"

"Dad says flight is the safest and most efficient way to travel across the country," he says. "I was scared because I've never flown before, but I just closed my eyes the whole time and squeezed a stress ball that my mom gave me. I think I squeezed it too hard. My hands hurt."

"No trouble with the taxi?" Mom says.

"The driver was there waiting for me like you said he would be. He even put on *Science Daily* for me. Hey, do you know the difference between a swamp and a bog?"

"Nope," says Mom. "Peter, why don't you help Tommy get settled? Dinner will be ready in a few minutes. I hope you like stir-fry, Tommy!"

"I like anything," says Tommy, which isn't true. He hates olives and blue cheese, and he doesn't like peanuts unless they're honey roasted. I know these things because he's my best friend.

When Mom goes back to the kitchen, I go back to staring at Tommy. Except, after a few seconds, I have to shut my eyes tight, because I'm feeling too many things at once—surprise, and confusion, and guilt.

Happiness, too. Mostly happiness.

Everyone talks about happiness like it's the best feeling ever, but sometimes happiness hits you like a wrecking ball and you need a moment to recover.

"Um, Peter, I know you're doing your deep breathing," says Tommy, "but my backpack is really heavy."

I open my eyes. Tommy is still there. Whew.

I grab his backpack so I can be a good host and carry it to my room, and he's not kidding. It's heavier than a sandbag! "What on earth did you pack?"

"My first aid kit, my wilderness survival kit, my zombie apocalypse survival kit, and some clothes. Oh, and the Discovery Journal."

I set the backpack in my room next to the leaky beanbag chair. "The Discovery Journal?"

"I thought we could finish it while I'm here," he says. "If there's time, I mean. I know the Indigo River Boating Club meeting is on Saturday."

A thousand *but*s fill my head. But I'm done with all that. But the Discovery Club doesn't exist anymore. But I'm not even going to the Indigo River Boating Club meeting.

I don't say any of those *but*s, though. I just poke Tommy in the arm.

"What was that for?" he says.

"Just making sure you're real."

"According to *Science Daily*, there's no scientific consensus on what reality is. If you mean that I'm corporeally real—"

Before he can finish that dumb sentence, I hug him.

THIRTY-TWO

Tommy and I go back to my room after dinner. I lie on my bed and Tommy lies on an air mattress that Mom inflated for him and he tells me everything—how he listened to *Science Daily* episodes the whole drive from Florida to Michigan; how he and his parents ate at a restaurant in Nashville where a woman with a guitar sang songs about heartache and whiskey; how Michigan feels cold compared to Florida, even though it's summer there, too, and actually pretty warm.

"We aren't near any bodies of water, at least," he says. "So the odds of me dying in a rip current are low."

I don't laugh because that would be mean. But then Tommy laughs, so I laugh a little bit, too.

After the laughter it's quiet. The sun just set and my room is growing dark, so I reach over to my nightstand and turn on the kaleidoscope lamp that Papa and I made years ago in his watch shop—the Dizzy Disco Kaleidoscope Lamp, to be exact. The lampshade has a bunch of different colors and patterns, and it spins when the lamp is turned on. For a few minutes I watch the colors dance across the ceiling. I think Tommy is watching them, too.

But I know I can't stay quiet forever. There's something I need to say. I'm having a hard time saying it, which is weird. I usually don't have a hard time saying anything. Usually I can't *stop* myself from saying things. It's a real problem.

Maybe this would be easier if my stomach would stop flip-flopping, or if my heart would stop tap-dancing, or if my palms would stop sweating. But I don't think any of those things are going to happen until I say what I need to say.

So I'm just going to say it now.

Seriously, I am.

Deep breath.

Here I go.

Wait. One more deep breath.

Okay, I'm *really* ready now.

"Tommy, I'm sorry."

I count the seconds of silence as they pass. By the time I get to seven, I can't take it anymore, so I just keep talking.

"I'm sorry I was such a bad friend when we said good-bye. I'm sorry I *couldn't* say goodbye. I was sad. I think I was sadder than I'd ever been in my whole entire life. Sometimes when I'm sad, I get mad—except I'm not *really* mad. I think I'm just sad. Does that make any sense?

"Also, I meant it when I told you to avoid rip currents in Michigan. I wasn't being sarcastic. Okay, maybe I *was* being sarcastic, but I really don't want you to get carried out to sea. That would be the worst thing ever. The point is, I'm sorry. Really sorry. So sorry it's killing me. Not literally, but . . . maybe literally."

I catch my breath. It's silent again. Well, except for my heart, which is beating so loud Tommy must be able to hear it. The whole world can probably hear it. Maybe even the whole galaxy.

"Can you please say something? You can say: 'I don't forgive you, Peter, because you're a real jerk.' Or: 'It's too late for sorry and I'll probably hate you for the rest of time, plus some more time after that.'"

Blue-green waves wash across the ceiling. This time I count all the way up to twenty-three seconds before Tommy says anything. It might just be the most stressful twenty-three seconds of my life.

"It hurt," he says finally. "A lot."

Okay, maybe it was better *before* he said anything. Now my allergies are flaring up. My eyes pool with water, blurring the edges of the colors slow-dancing around my room. I want to burrow under my covers and disappear.

"I don't think you're a jerk, though," he says. "You did *act* like a jerk. But that doesn't mean you *are* a jerk."

I knuckle my eyes and turn on my side to face Tommy. "I'm pretty sure that *is* what that means."

"But Peter, that's like saying that just because you baked a cake once, you're a baker. Or, because you went fishing once, you're a fisherman. Or—"

"So you *don't* hate me?"

Tommy closes his eyes. At first I wonder if he fell asleep, which would be the worst timing ever, but then he says: "I was mad at you, Peter. Really mad. It was hard. I don't like being mad. It's my least favorite feeling ever." He pauses. "But I don't hate you. I could never hate you."

"That's just because you could never hate anyone," I say.

His eyes blink open. He looks at me through all of the colors. "I especially could never hate you."

Ugh. I don't get it. How is Tommy so nice? How is it even *possible* to be so nice? It's too much. My allergies are on fire.

"Why are you here?" I say. "I'm *glad* you're here—really glad—but I don't know *why.*"

"Your mom called my mom—"

"I know, but *why* did she call?"

Tommy's skin turns from blue to purple in the lamplight.

"She said that your grandpa was at a rehabilitation center and that you could use a friend."

I hold up my hand to catch a swirl of red light. "I'm fine," I say.

"But, Peter . . ."

"What?"

"When you said 'I'm fine,' your voice jumped a few pitches. That's one of the telltale signs that someone is lying. *Science Daily* did an episode on lie detection, which was part of their *So You Wanna Be a Criminal Investigator?* series, which I listened to on the drive to Michigan when I was feeling really mad at you."

I grab a pillow and hold it tight to my chest, right over my heart. Maybe Tommy's right. Maybe I'm not fine. Maybe I haven't been fine for a while.

"Papa is sick and it's not just his hip."

I feel lighter after I say it, like I've been carrying a stone inside of me and I just spit it out.

But I feel scared, too. Part of me wants to gobble the stone back up.

It's too late now, though. And deep down I know I should have told Tommy this a while ago.

So now I tell him everything—why Papa moved in with us, and why I stopped inviting Tommy over to my house. I tell him about Official Caregiver Duty and how I messed it all up.

"He only walked out into that storm because of me. I filled his head with manatees, and told him we could build a Marvelous Manatee Storm Sanctuary together, and left him alone in the kitchen when he was confused. He fell because of me. He's hurt right now because of me."

I've thought these words a million times over the last month, but they feel different out loud. They feel truer. I bury my face in the pillow.

"I don't think you're to blame for what happened to your grandpa," says Tommy. "You might be feeling hyper-responsibility, which is this psychological thing where someone overestimates the role they played in something bad that happened. I learned about it on—"

I peek my eyes over the pillow. *"Science Daily?"*

Tommy nods. "And just because something bad happened, that doesn't mean you're a bad caretaker. You can't control *everything*, can you?"

"Shh," I say, because the more Tommy talks, the more my eyes burn.

"Allergies?" he says.

I want to say yes. I want to make a joke about how I'm allergic to Tommy being such a dork and using words like *hyper-responsibility*. But today is a day for telling the truth. "I don't have allergies and you know it."

"I always wondered why your only allergy symptom was watery eyes. When I get allergies, my nose runs a lot and I sneeze and sometimes my hearing goes funny. Mom wants me to get allergy shots, but . . ."

But he's afraid of shots. I know things like this because he's my best friend.

I sit up and try to wipe away the tears running down my face, but there's too many and I can't catch them all. I think I'm crying a whole summer's worth of tears. Maybe eleven years' worth of tears. So I stop trying to catch them. I just let them go, the way Tommy does.

"I'm not going to the Indigo River Boating Club meeting," I say.

Now Tommy sits up, too. "Peter, you *have* to go to the meeting."

It's pretty weird to hear Tommy say that I *have* to do something. Tommy never tells me what I *have* to do.

"It was a stupid idea," I say. "It's just going to cause trouble."

"But you're not afraid of trouble. Peter, you're the bravest person I know. You might be the bravest person I'll ever know. It's hard to say, because I don't know who all I'll meet in my life, but . . . you're definitely in the bravest subset of human beings."

I shake my head. I feel like a snotty, swollen mess. "The meeting is in five days. I haven't even memorized my speech, and the poster . . . went missing."

Today might be a day for telling the truth, but I'm not

telling Tommy about jumping up and down on the poster in the recycling bin. That's just embarrassing.

"But I can help," says Tommy. "We can spend the rest of the week preparing."

I rack my brain for more excuses. If I speak at the meeting, I'll definitely tick off Mr. Reilly, and he might stop working with Mom. But then I remember what Mom said a few weeks ago: *If you change your mind about the meeting, just know that I'll support you.*

As the lamp keeps spinning and my skin turns every color of the rainbow, I think about how weird it's felt to not be planning big, exciting things this past month. I'm *always* planning big, exciting things.

I think about Zoe's cut—how deep it was, and how red, and how it made *me* hurt just to look at it.

I think about all the work Tommy and I put into building a watertight case for why boaters should help take care of manatees.

I think about how Tommy just said I'm the bravest person he knows. I liked that. I liked that a lot.

Now my heart is dancing again but not in a bad, jittery way. In a good way. In a time-to-get-to-work way.

Tommy gives me a nod and I give him a smile. I think it's my first real smile in weeks. It feels strange at first, like I'm using a muscle that's been asleep for a while, but then it feels just right.

While Tommy watches, I grab my phone from my nightstand and dial the number for the Florida Manatee Society. Nobody picks up. Maybe because it's nighttime. Oh well. I'll just leave a message after the beep.

BEEP!

"Cassidy Cawley, it's Peter. I'm back in."

THIRTY-THREE

The Indigo River Boating Club meeting isn't exactly how I imagined it.

I thought there would be a huge auditorium with a brightly lit stage and hundreds of people in the audience, ready to listen to me and nod along and maybe cry a little bit while I said super inspirational and persuasive things.

But the meeting is actually being held inside a big shed at the marina, and there are only about thirty people here, and that includes me, Tommy, Cassidy, Billy, Maria, and a few others from the Florida Manatee Society. Instead of fancy auditorium seats, there are folding chairs, and there isn't even a stage. Mr. Reilly is just sitting on a flimsy table at the front of the shed as he announces that the club's annual membership fee is increasing by 12 percent. This earns him some grumbles from the crowd.

"All renewing members get an Indigo River Boating Club tote bag and a ten-dollar coupon for Barry's Boat Warehouse!" he says. Not exactly the deal of a lifetime.

"Psst," I whisper to Cassidy. "This isn't how I pictured it."

"I know," she whispers back. "Who knew there'd be so many people here?!"

Huh. I guess Cassidy and I had very different expectations for this meeting.

I'm a little worried about her. She's been shaking and sweating ever since we sat down. Actually, she's been shaking and sweating ever since we gathered at the Florida Manatee Society office before the meeting to eat doughnuts and carpool to the marina. And now I'm wondering if her nerves are contagious because I can't stop tapping my foot on the concrete floor of the shed, and my stomach feels like it's full of wriggling earthworms.

Cassidy glances at Billy. He gives her a thumbs-up. She smiles, but she still looks seasick. Maybe doughnuts were a bad idea, even though they were totally delicious.

"Fresh air," Cassidy murmurs. Then she slips out of the shed.

Up front, Mr. Reilly clears his throat. "Now, a small matter of business. We won't be voting on the next president at this meeting as originally planned. The club secretaries have decided that presidents should serve for two and a half years instead of two." He sighs. I don't trust the sigh. "This job is a *lot* of work and I'm a very busy man, but I told them I'll keep serving the club as long as I'm needed."

The audience stirs. The grumbles get louder. I would grumble along with them—I mean, who wants more President Reilly?—but my foot is still tap-tap-tapping and the earthworms are still wriggling and I've got other things on my mind.

I lean over to Tommy. "Do you think my speech covers everything? Should I talk about other manatee species, like the kind of manatee that lives down in the Amazon? Do you think we have enough information about how to report an injured manatee?"

"The speech is great, Falcon," Tommy says. "We included lots of pertinent data."

"Okay," I say, "but I still don't know what *pertinent* means."

"*Pertinent* is a synonym for relevant, or—"

Tommy freezes. Mr. Reilly is glaring at us. A few of the boaters follow his gaze. They're mostly men about Mr. Reilly's age with sunburnt, whiskery faces, but there are a few women, too. No Mrs. Reilly.

I sit up tall and give Mr. Reilly my I'm-not-afraid-of-you face.

Except . . . I think I *am* afraid. Not of Mr. Reilly, though.

Not of public speaking, either—I've got no problem with that. I'm pretty sure I could speak to a whole football stadium without breaking a sweat.

So . . . I don't know what it is.

I look at the shed door. Cassidy is still outside. No sign of Mom yet. She had to show a house this morning, but she said she would be here. She said she wouldn't miss it.

"That's it for today's business," Mr. Reilly says, hopping off the table and stretching his back until it cracks loud enough for everyone in the shed to hear. "If you want to stick around, we've got some guests here again from the whaddya call it . . . the Manatee Gang."

Boy, it takes all my effort not to scream *Florida Manatee Society!* at the top of my lungs.

"Or we could hit the water," Mr. Reilly says. "Beautiful day outside, boys! And, uh, ladies."

Some boaters look back at us. Others start making their way for the door. But before anyone leaves, Maria stands. "Please do stick around," she says. "We'll just borrow a few minutes of your time."

Her voice is a bell, bright but firm. The room quiets and the boaters who stood up sit back down. Mr. Reilly glowers at Maria as she steps in front of him and turns to face the crowd.

"First of all, thanks for having us. I believe I've met some of you before, but let me introduce myself: My name is Maria Liu, and I'm the president of the Florida Manatee Society." With a small smile, she draws out the name of the organization long and slow so Mr. Reilly can't miss it. "We're a nonprofit organization dedicated to manatee conservation. Today, we just want to go over a few ways that we can all work together to protect the manatees that live in the Indigo River."

As I listen to Maria, I think I get why Cassidy looks up to her so much. She seems so confident and calm. Maria has studied manatees her whole life, according to Cassidy, and she started working for the Florida Manatee Society years before Tommy and I were even born. But even though Maria cares about manatees more than anything, she isn't yelling at the boaters or accusing them of anything. She's talking to them like they're her friends. Like they really might be interested in protecting manatees if they have the facts.

So she gives them the facts. She talks about the current state of the West Indian manatee population. She talks about how many manatees are injured each year in boating strikes and the average number of scars on a manatee's back. And I still think Maria is a very impressive person, but now I also think Maria is a slightly annoying person.

"I was going to say all that!" I hiss in Tommy's ear.

He points at the speech in my hands, the one we typed up and printed this morning. "Maybe just cut this paragraph? And . . . maybe this one, too."

I frown. "Be right back," I say. Then I tiptoe to the door so I won't disturb Maria's presentation.

Outside, the sun is bright and the air smells like salt and fish. Boats bob in the water and knock against wooden docks. I spy Cassidy sitting cross-legged on the dock closest to the shed, looking out across the river.

I hurry over. "Maria is taking some of the points I was going to make in my speech, so I need to know what you're planning to—"

I stop when I see her face. I expected her to be shaking and sweating. I didn't expect her to be crying.

"I can't do this," she says. "I just *can't* do this."

"That's perfect!" Wait. That didn't sound right. "I mean, my speech is very comprehensive, so if you don't want to speak, you don't have to."

She shakes her head. "I'm not just talking about the speech, Peter. I'm talking about this job."

"What do you mean?"

She draws her knees up to her chest. "It was okay when I was an intern. But now it's a real job, and I never know if I'm doing enough, or doing it right, or if I'm just in everyone's way."

"Don't you like working with manatees?"

"Of course! But what if I'm not like Maria? What if I don't want to devote my whole life to this? What if I want to study something else at some point, or go back to school, or work with another animal, or . . . I don't know! Join the circus."

I sit down next to her. Below us, minnows dart around the barnacle-covered posts of the dock. They're so tiny.

"Cassidy Cawley, are you good at juggling?"

She rests her cheek on her knees and looks at me like a sad sideways fish. "No," she says miserably. "The circus probably wouldn't even take me."

"What about metaphorical juggling?"

"Huh?"

"A metaphor is a figure of speech where—"

"I know what a metaphor is," she says. I think she's smiling, but it's hard to tell because her face is smushed.

I take off my flip-flops and dangle my feet in the water, letting the minnows tickle my toes. "Do you ever feel like you're juggling way too many things and you just keep dropping the balls, no matter how hard you try to keep them all in the air?"

"Yes," Cassidy says. "All the time. Every day. Since I was like . . . seven."

I wiggle my toes. The minnows scatter, then come right back. "Well," I say, "I know what that's like."

Cassidy lifts her chin and looks out across the water again. A speedboat flies past, drawing a choppy wake down the middle of the river.

"Can I tell you something embarrassing?" Cassidy says.

"Always," I say, trying not to sound *too* eager.

"I didn't want college to end. My friends were so excited for graduation, so I thought I should be, too. But I was scared. I felt like it was ending just as I was getting used to it. Or getting *good* at it." She looks down at her bright purple sneakers and gives the laces a tug. "I've always been scared of change. Even if it's good change, like getting my dream job working for the Florida Manatee Society. Does that make any sense? Or am I just weird?"

In my mind I picture Carter Middle School looming like a dark fortress on a craggy mountain peak. Which is strange, because Mom and I have driven by Carter lots of times and it's actually a one-story brick building across from a strip mall.

Still, I shiver. There's a cold wind blowing down from that imaginary mountain.

"If you're weird," I say, "I think we're the same kind of weird."

"I had a hunch that might be the case," says Cassidy.

"You're great at your job, though. You helped save Zoe. You always answer the phone, even during a Category 3 hurricane. And . . ." I sigh. "You really should speak to those boaters. Even if you take the rest of my points. And even if you're scared.

"You can try my one-thing-at-a-time strategy. Right

227

now, the only thing you need to focus on is getting up in front of that shed. Everything else we can figure out later. Even the circus."

We sit quietly for a minute. I wonder if Maria is waiting on us. I wonder why I still feel so jittery. Cassidy's nerves *must* be contagious.

"Fine," she says finally. "But I better not throw up in front of Billy."

"It doesn't matter," I say. "He'll still have a crush on you."

She scowls, but she smiles, too. "Hey, thanks for the pep talk."

"I'm very motivating," I say.

When we get back inside, Maria waves Cassidy to the front of the shed and introduces her. Billy gives her another thumbs-up. I don't really believe in telepathy, but just in case it's real, I send her a message: *You've got this.*

"Right," Cassidy says. "So, there are a few things you can do—I mean, we can *all* do—to help keep manatees safe."

Her voice starts out wobbly, but as she talks about the importance of obeying low-speed zones while boating, and not littering, and how to report an injured manatee, her voice grows stronger and stronger. Maybe she got my telepathic message after all. I'm so proud of her, even though she's totally taking the rest of my points.

"There goes the whole second part of my speech," I whisper.

"She hasn't mentioned polarized sunglasses," Tommy whispers back.

"I can't give a whole speech on polarized sunglasses!"

Sweat trickles down my face. My heart rattles. What am I going to do?

Maybe I can write another speech before it's my turn. Maybe I can make it a poem, or a song, or a stand-up comedy routine, or . . . something original. Something *amazing.*

But by the time Tommy fishes a stubby pencil out of one of his cargo shorts pockets, Cassidy is already wrapping up. "Before we go," she says, "a friend of mine named Peter wants to share a few words. He's a young activist."

Activist. I like that. I really like that. But I still have no idea what I'm going to say.

"You'll figure something out, Falcon," Tommy says. "You always do."

"Thanks, Fox." I hope he's right.

As I take Cassidy's place at the front of the shed, Mr. Reilly looks at me the same way he looked at me when he caught me stealing avocados in his backyard last summer. Like I'm a tiny bug he wants to squash. I ignore him and focus on the crowd.

Every face is looking at me. Tommy is holding up his phone to record me, just like we planned. Cassidy and Maria and Billy are all smiling in an encouraging sort of way.

Still no Mom, though. I really thought she'd be here. Maybe if I wait just a little bit longer . . .

I hear the pop of Mr. Reilly's jaw behind me. He must be chewing his invisible tobacco again. Ugh. I need to start talking *now*, if only to drown him out.

"I'm here to tell you all about the benefits of polarized sunglasses," I say.

Or, at least, that's what I start to say. Before I can finish, the shed door creaks open. Sunlight pours in, so blinding that I can't see who's entering at first, but I hear the click-clack of her high heels on the concrete. I would know that click-clack anywhere. She's here. She made it. And she's not alone. Behind her is . . . Dexter? He's pushing a wheelchair, and sitting in the wheelchair . . .

I can't believe it.

I really can't believe it.

"You know, these meetings aren't just open to the public," Mr. Reilly grumbles, but I don't care, because Dexter is parking Papa's wheelchair next to Tommy, and Mom is hurrying toward me, carrying something in her arms. Something big. Something colorful.

"I found this in the recycling a few weeks ago," she whispers, setting my visual aid on the table behind me. "I thought I'd save it, just in case."

The colors on the poster are still streaked from when I carried it home from Tommy's house in the rain, and it's a little bent and wobbly, I guess from all the times I jumped on it to get it to fit in the recycling bin. But it looks like Mom tried to flatten it out.

"I'm so sorry I'm late," she whispers. "It took a while to pick up Papa, and I really wanted him to be here."

I don't know what to say. All I can manage is, "I was just getting started."

"Marianne, I warned you—" Mr. Reilly begins.

"Not now," Mom snaps. Boy, it's nice, hearing her snap at Mr. Reilly like that. She takes a seat by Papa and Tommy, and that's when I realize that everyone I love is in the same room at the same time.

The meeting still isn't exactly how I imagined it, though. Tommy and Papa might be here, but Tommy is only visiting, and Papa looks lost. I can't catch his eyes. Mom holds one of his hands and Dexter holds the other, like he might float away if they don't.

As I look from Tommy to Papa, it finally dawns on me why I'm nervous.

I thought I could do everything this summer. I thought I could be the best caretaker in the world, and finally finish the Discovery Journal, and find a way to keep Tommy here, too. But I couldn't do any of it.

So maybe I can't help the manatees, either. Maybe there's nothing I can say right now that will make a difference to these boaters.

And even if I can make a difference, it won't fix *every-thing*. After this meeting, manatees will still be at risk. Animals all over the world will still be at risk. The problem is too big—so big it might just swallow me whole.

You're definitely in the bravest subset of human beings. That's what Tommy said. I don't know, though. Right now I don't feel very brave. I feel scared. And small.

But I'm here. I'm standing in front of a crowd waiting to hear me speak. I have an eye-catching visual aid. I have a best friend recording me.

I have to say *something*.

I have to try.

I take a deep breath, the way Mom taught me—inhale until my lungs can't hold any more, exhale until they're completely empty. I look at Papa. Finally, he looks at me, too. Then I start talking.

"When my Papa—that's him, right there—when he was my age, he was out in the Indigo River one day trying to catch some fish. And instead of fish, he found a manatee."

I know the story by heart, which is a funny expression. It's not like Papa's story is actually stored somewhere in my heart, between the ventricles or beneath the aorta. (Tommy once made me listen to an episode of *Science Daily* about the heart.) I think when we talk about our hearts, we really mean our brains. Except, a lot of the time I do feel things in my chest, right where my heart is. I wonder if Tommy knows why.

"He followed the manatee to a cove," I say, "where he found another manatee, and then another, and another, until he realized there was a whole herd of manatees swimming there, all around him."

It's weird to be telling Papa his own story. It feels backward. But it looks like he's listening—like he's waiting to hear what happens next—and I swear I see the hint of a crooked smile on his face.

So I keep going. I tell everyone how he stayed there in the cove until sunset with the manatees, and how he felt peaceful, like there was nowhere else he needed to be and nothing else he needed to do.

"When I met a manatee, that's how I felt, too," I say.

I explain how Tommy and I formed the Discovery Club, and how Zoe was Discovery #95.

"She was *huge*. Way bigger than I thought a manatee could be. But she was gentle, too. She never tried to hurt us. She was calm, and she made *me* feel calm, which is— well, that's saying something."

I see Mom smile.

"But then she got hurt. A boat hit her, and—"

"Objection!" says Mr. Reilly. "You don't know it was a boat."

"All signs pointed to a boating strike," says Cassidy. I guess she surprised herself, though, because she quickly clamps her hands over her mouth.

"The laceration was consistent with what we've seen in other manatees injured from boating collisions," Maria adds calmly.

"And I've treated a whole lot of manatees," Billy says. "I know a boating injury when I see one."

"But you can't say that one of us did it," says Mr. Reilly, glaring at me. Not Cassidy. Not Maria. Not Billy. Me. "You didn't *see* it, did you?"

"Mr. Reilly, let my son finish."

Every head turns to the woman who just spoke. The woman who basically just told Mr. Reilly to shut up, even though he's buying up every property in town and he might be her only shot at Space Coast Real Estate Agent of the Year. My mom. My awesome, tough, kind-of-scary-when-she's-mad mom.

"I'm the president of this club," Mr. Reilly barks, "and I'll speak when I feel like it."

I take another deep breath because what I'm about to say isn't going to be easy. "Mr. Reilly is right."

Mom stares at me in shock. So does Mr. Reilly.

"Not about being president, though I guess you're right about that, too," I say. "But what I mean is, you're right that I didn't see who hit Zoe. So maybe I shouldn't have pointed at you on the news, even though the video went viral and made me famous—well, locally famous—and that was

234

pretty cool. Really cool, actually.

"But *somebody* hit Zoe. And maybe that somebody didn't mean to hurt a manatee, but now she's at a rehabilitation center with a punctured lung and a new scar." I look directly at Mr. Reilly. "So . . . this isn't about you."

I figured he would be happy that I'm giving him a break. Isn't this what he wanted? But he doesn't look happy. He looks angry, and flustered, and . . . something else. Something I don't recognize.

I turn back to the audience. "What I'm trying to say is, it's about all of us. We should all try to keep manatees safe, because they're living creatures, just like us. We shouldn't ignore them or let them get hurt. We should be caretakers."

I feel like I should be moving toward the conclusion now—Tommy says watertight cases need good conclusions—but it's hard without a speech to read from.

"So . . . please help. Because one person can make a difference, but lots of people can probably make lots of difference."

Okay, that sounds pretty conclusive to me. I'm about to walk back to my seat, but then I have another thought.

"Actually, we should protect *all* animals. All the birds and fish and lizards and everything. But it's really overwhelming to focus on a million things at once—it can make you feel like your head is going to explode, trust me—so I'm starting with manatees and maybe you can start with manatees, too."

This time, before I leave, I wait a moment to make sure there's really nothing else I need to say.

"Okay. I'm done now."

A few people clap. It's not a whole auditorium of people cheering for me the way I imagined it, but it still feels pretty good.

And it feels even better when I see Papa shake off Mom's and Dexter's hands so he can clap, too.

THIRTY-FOUR

Some of the boaters leave as soon as my speech is over, but others stick around to talk to the Florida Manatee Society team. A few of them talk to me, too. They thank me for speaking and tell me about times they've spotted manatees in the Indigo River. They say they want to help.

"I always keep an eye out for them," says a woman with a lobster-red sunburn. "They're just so hard to spot sometimes."

I remind her about polarized sunglasses. *"P-O-L-A-R-I-Z-E-D,"* I say.

"I know how to spell *polarized*, dear."

I figured all the boaters would be like Mr. Reilly and not care about manatees. But some of them *do* care. And some of them don't seem to think all that much of Mr. Reilly.

"That video of you pointing at Eddie is *classic*," says a man with a Miami Marlins baseball cap.

"Isn't he your president?" I say.

The man snorts. "He was supposed to be stepping down soon. Lord knows what he was talking about today. I don't think this club even has secretaries!" He leans in conspiratorially. "But to tell you the truth, Eddie's had a rough go of it lately. So maybe we can let him have this one."

"You mean because Mrs. Reilly is divorcing him?"

The man nods. "Poor guy can't get anyone to stick around. His own kids won't even have anything to do with him."

"Wait—Mr. and Mrs. Reilly have *kids*?"

"Eddie does. A son and a daughter, I think, from his first marriage. His last wife up and left one day and took the kids with her. That was years ago. Now it looks like family number two isn't working out so hot, either."

The man turns to chat up somebody else. I stand frozen to the spot, letting this sink in. Then I scan the shed for Mr. Reilly.

There's Tommy, sitting with Papa and Dexter.

There's Maria and Cassidy and Billy, handing out Florida Manatee Society brochures to boaters as they leave.

And there he is. Mr. Reilly. My archnemesis. He's leering

over Mom, jabbing a finger in her face, talking fast. I strain to catch his voice through all the chatter in the shed: "I told you if your son kept causing trouble, I'd find another agent for my properties, and I intend to do just that."

I storm toward them, getting ready to tell Mr. Reilly off. I might be done trying to embarrass him on the local news, but I'm not letting him talk to Mom this way, even if he's had a "rough go of it lately."

But I don't have to tell him off. Mom beats me to the punch.

"Please do find another agent," she says. "Honestly, I'm not interested in doing business with you anymore, Eddie. And I swear to God, if you say another word to me about my son—or if you don't get your finger out of my face— you are *not* going to like what happens next."

I watch them stare each other down. Mr. Reilly is a lot taller than Mom, but right now it doesn't look like it. Maybe it's the way Mom has her feet planted, or the way she's jutting out her chin and staring up at him like she's just daring him to make her angrier.

Or maybe it's that look on his face, the one I don't recognize. I tilt my head and squint. Beneath his sneer, he looks tired. And . . . sad?

It's weird seeing new things in an old face. It makes you wonder if those things have been there all along and you've just been missing them.

Mr. Reilly looks around like he's searching for something, but whatever it is, he must not find it. He storms out of the shed, ignoring Cassidy when she offers him a Florida Manatee Society brochure. If he recognizes her as the girl who almost ran him over on my street, he doesn't say anything.

"Hi," I say, startling Mom.

She pulls me close. "I'm so proud of you, Peter."

The words are fireflies in my heart, lighting me up from the inside. I want to linger in this moment—I'm afraid if I say anything, it'll break the spell—but I'm suddenly full of questions and I can't keep them in.

"But is Mr. Reilly really going to use a different agent? And if he does, how much longer will you have to work before you can take time off again? And what are we going to do about Papa when I go back to school?"

Mom looks across the shed at Papa. Worry lines crinkle her face, and I think about how hard this must have been for her, to bring Papa somewhere new and strange, when all she wants to do is keep him safe.

Maybe Mom is in the bravest subset of human beings, too.

"When Papa comes home, he's going to need full-time care," she says. "Even more than before. So I'm scheduling some interviews with professional caregivers. I figure I can keep working a few days a week, at least, and we can have someone be with Papa when I can't."

"What if he doesn't like the caregiver? What if the caregiver doesn't understand him? What if—"

"Peter," Mom says. She places her hands on my shoulders and looks me square in the eye. "I'm going to be honest with you, okay? I don't know how this is all going to play out. And I hate that. I really hate it. But all we can do right now is take it a day at a time."

She doesn't let go of my shoulders or look away. The rest of the shed fades into the background, and it's just me and Mom, on our own little island. It's nice to have some company. It's nice to feel like a team again.

"When you got knocked out during that storm, Peter, that was the scariest day of my life. Every day when I see you, I'm just so glad to *see* you." She gives me a little shake. "And if we got through that, then I'm betting we can get through anything. Especially if we get a little help. Okay?"

"Okay," I say. "And . . . thank you."

Really, I need to say a lot of thank-yous to Mom—thank you for coming to the meeting, and for bringing Papa and my visual aid, and for arranging Tommy's visit, and for finally standing up to Mr. Reilly.

"Times a million," I add. Hopefully that covers it.

"Thank *you*, Peter." I don't know what she's thanking me for, but I decide not to ask. I decide to just enjoy it.

"By the way," she says as we walk toward Papa, "I told your dad about this meeting."

"You talked to Dad again?"

"He called to check in a few days ago. I told him you were giving a speech. He was excited for you."

"Dad was *excited*?"

"Well . . . in his own way. Maybe you can update him? Let him know how it went?"

I must look pretty confused, because Mom rubs my shoulder and says, "No pressure. Never any pressure. Just think about it."

"Okay," I say. "I will."

After all the boaters leave, I introduce Cassidy and Maria and Billy to Mom and Papa and Dexter. I forgot that Cassidy already met Mom when she came to our house to pick me up for Emerald Springs. There are suddenly a lot of people in my life—a lot more than I'm used to, anyway—and it's hard to keep track of who knows who, but right now they all get to know each other, which is weird and awesome.

I guess it's too many people for Tommy, though, because he hides behind me like I'm one of the bushes outside Mr. Reilly's old house.

"I recorded your whole speech, Falcon," he whispers. "I got the clapping at the end, too."

"Thanks, Fox," I say, even though the whole point of

Tommy recording my speech was so I could show it to Papa later. And now I don't need to, because Papa's here. But who knows? Maybe I'll upload it on YouTube and go viral again.

Maybe I'll send it to Dad, too. I don't know if I want to talk to him, but . . . he could watch the video, at least. I mean, if he wants.

While everyone else is talking, I scooch closer to Papa. I'm not sure he understands everything that's going on, but he smiles a lot, and when we laugh, he laughs, too. I think he's having what Dexter would call a "better" day. I know it might not last, but that just makes it feel really special right now.

And honestly, after trying to keep his dementia a secret for so long, it's a relief to have everyone meet him. To *see* him.

When it's time to leave the shed, I ask Dexter if I can wheel Papa back to the car. I push the chair slowly, letting the others move ahead of us so for a minute, at least, it's just me and Papa.

"I'm really glad you were here," I say.

"Wouldn't have missed it for the world," says Papa. He looks at me over his shoulder and smiles mischievously. "Though you missed part of my story, you know."

"I did? Which part?"

"I jumped into the water. I swam with them, Peter. I swam with the manatees."

Papa has never mentioned swimming with the manatees before. But right now his eyes are clear, and his bushy brows are waggling, and he remembers my name, and I believe him. I believe all of it.

THIRTY-FIVE

By the time the Channel 9 van pulls into the neighborhood, there's already a crowd gathered by the canal, and the steamy air is buzzing with anticipation. And mosquitos. Lots of mosquitos.

It's the first day of August—two days after the Indigo River Boating Club meeting, two days before Tommy flies back to Michigan, and one week before my first day at Carter Middle School. The sun is blazing, so Tommy and I huddle in the shade of a palm tree while we wait for Zoe to arrive.

There are way more people here than I expected. According to Maria Liu, this is one of the most anticipated manatee releases in years, thanks to all the local news coverage of Zoe's rescue. Nearby, Mom is chatting with Maria and Cassidy. I spot Mrs. Reilly in the crowd, too. When she sees me and Tommy, she drifts our way.

"Isn't this exciting, boys? I'm staying at my sister's house across town, but I just had to swing by." She blinks at Tommy. "Didn't you move?"

"Yes, ma'am," he says. "I'm just visiting."

"Well, that's nice!" She smiles in a distracted sort of way. Shielding her eyes from the sun with her hands, she looks down the canal at Tommy's house. I mean, Tommy's *old* house. "I guess he's all moved in there now, isn't he? Well, I hope it makes him happy, having the biggest house in the neighborhood. God knows it's what he wanted."

I think about the look on Mr. Reilly's face at the boating club meeting. I'm not sure the big house did the trick.

"After that poor manatee got hurt," Mrs. Reilly goes on, "I told Eddie to take it easy with the motorboat. I even bought him a canoe." She points to a shiny red canoe lying in the grass near the dock of Tommy's old house. I hadn't noticed it till now. "Doubt he's used it." She shakes her head, then turns away to talk to some of the other neighbors.

"Don't *ever* let me get married," I tell Tommy.

"Okay," says Tommy. "I'll do my best."

We watch the Channel 9 team set up. I spy the reporter who interviewed me back when Zoe was rescued—the same reporter who said that driving during Hurricane Bernard was sheer madness. I'm glad he survived the storm.

Then, finally, another van turns into the neighborhood—a Florida Marine Life Commission van.

A hush falls over the crowd. She's here. After almost two months of rehabilitation, of watch and wait, of liquid food injections and learning how to swim again, Zoe is being released back into the wild.

When Cassidy called yesterday to tell me the news, I was scared to believe her. I didn't want to get my hopes up in case something fell through. But now it's really happening.

We all make room for the van to back up to the edge of the canal. When the van doors swing open, I catch a glimpse of Zoe, lying on a blue tarp between Billy and a few others who made the trip from Emerald Springs with her.

This time, I refuse to watch from the sidelines. I weave my way to the front of the crowd so I can join the people climbing into the back of the van to lift Zoe. I expect Mom to tell me to stay back, but instead, she joins me. So does Cassidy. We all cram into the van like sardines, finding spots along the edge of the tarp.

"You sure you're up for this?" Billy asks me. "She's pretty heavy!"

"I'm tough," I say, puffing out my chest.

"Glad to have you on board, then! Alright, everyone, on the count of three. One . . ."

My eyes trace the new scar on Zoe's back. It's white now, like the rest. I think about what Cassidy told me on the phone yesterday—that Zoe might never swim exactly like she used to. She healed, but not perfectly.

"Two . . ."

I wish Papa could be here. We'd planned on it—Mom was supposed to pick him and Dexter up from Dogwood this morning so he could watch Zoe's release. But Dexter called earlier and said that Papa was too confused today to make the trip. Channel 9 better be getting some good footage for him.

"Three!"

We grab the tarp and lift. "AHHH!" I scream. I don't mean to scream, but I can't help it, because Billy wasn't kidding—Zoe is *heavy*! I mean, I knew manatees were heavy, but this is just ridiculous. "What have you been feeding her?!"

"Lots of romaine, baby!" Billy yells.

Okay, maybe I should've watched from the sidelines. But it's too late now—we're already shuffling down the ramp and splashing into the canal.

From the bank, Tommy and Mrs. Reilly cheer us on while the Channel 9 cameras roll. I flash the cameras a grin, like carrying a manatee is a piece of cake, even though I'm pretty sure my arms are about to pop out of their sockets.

But as we walk farther into the canal, Zoe gets lighter, and lighter, until . . .

She's in the water.

At first, she just floats above the tarp. Everyone is silent. Everyone is watching. Zoe is the center of the universe and we're all just orbiting her, waiting and hoping, frozen between one moment and the next.

Then, with a flick of her tail, she's off, swimming down the canal!

People cheer and scramble along the banks to follow her, taking pictures with their phones. The Channel 9 reporter is walking and talking as the cameras roll. I spy Cassidy and Billy hugging, waist-deep in the canal. It's their least awkward hug yet. I think they're making progress.

When Mom and I climb out of the canal, Tommy is waiting for us. "I'm sorry I didn't help," he says. "I was afraid to get in the water. Also, I have weak arms."

"That's okay, Fox." Usually Tommy's fear of water annoys me, but I'm just so glad he's here.

With Mom on our heels, Tommy and I dart through the crowd to keep pace with Zoe. She's a shimmering shadow beneath the water, moving fast—well, fast for a manatee, at least. Maybe she didn't heal perfectly, but it's not holding her back. And even though it's hot and loud and crowded, and I keep getting jostled by everyone, I get that feeling again as I watch her—a happy stillness in my heart.

I try to hold on to the feeling when the Channel 9 reporter finds me and sticks a microphone in my face. "You're the boy who found the manatee when she was injured, aren't you? How does it feel to see her released?"

Behind the camera, I see Tommy and Mom and Cassidy and Billy and Maria and Mrs. Reilly all watching me.

"It feels good," I say. "Really good."

"Are you still mad at the man who hit her with his boat?"

I think the Channel 9 news team wants another viral moment. I kind of want another viral moment, too. But I meant what I said at the Indigo River Boating Club meeting. This isn't about Mr. Reilly. It's not about me, either. Well, it's not *only* about me.

"We can all do our part to help the manatees," I say.

The reporter smiles politely, but he looks a little disappointed, too. The camera swings away from me. I probably won't go viral again.

But maybe Papa is watching Channel 9 at Dogwood right now. Maybe he saw me. Maybe his eyes just cleared.

THIRTY-SIX

It's nearly midnight when Tommy and I hear the screech.

We're lying on our stomachs on the floor of my bedroom, shoulder to shoulder, watching nature documentaries on Mom's laptop. I'm usually supposed to be in bed by ten, but Mom is making an exception while Tommy's here. Also, I never really go to bed at ten.

At first, I figure the screech is part of the video, but the documentary is about sharks and I'm pretty sure sharks don't screech.

Tommy hits pause, and there it is again: *SCREECH!*

Definitely real life, and very spine-tingling. "A bird?" I say.

Tommy nods. "I'm not sure what kind, though."

We crouch by the window and I raise the blinds, just a smidge, so we can peer outside. The moon and stars are bright tonight and my backyard is glowing. It becomes a game of who can spot the screecher first.

"There!" I say, but it's just a bush quivering in the wind.

"No—*there*," Tommy says.

I follow the direction of his finger, up to the highest branches of the tallest tree in the yard. A little face peeks out from the leaves, gleaming white, big eyes unblinking. An owl. The first owl I've ever seen in the wild—I mean, if my backyard counts as the wild.

I clamp my hands over my ears when it screeches again. "I thought owls were supposed to hoot."

Tommy is already looking up owls on Mom's laptop. "This appears to be a barn owl, judging by its face, which is shaped like an upside-down heart. Apparently, barn owls screech instead of hooting."

"This isn't a barn," I point out.

"It says here they can be found in many different environments, including the suburbs."

The suburban owl screeches again. I shiver. But not just because of the screech. "Tommy, do you know what this means?"

He nods gravely. "Discovery #100."

After Zoe's release this afternoon, Tommy and I were

too excited to relax, so Mom drove us to a state park for a walk through the woods. We hit the discovery jackpot, spotting a broadhead skink AND an eastern fence lizard, henceforth known as Discoveries #98 and #99. As soon we got home, we filled in the new entries, bringing us all the way up to 198 pages in our 200-page journal.

Now we huddle over the final two pages. While Tommy writes barn owl facts on the right page, I sketch on the left. The owl eventually flies away in a blur of wings and feathers, but we keep working until the pages are full. Until the journal is complete.

Afterward, we both stare at the pages for a long, long time.

Tommy and I worked on the Discovery Journal for three years. We promised each other we would finish it this summer, but when Tommy left, I thought it would never happen.

And then, just like that, it did.

Later, when Tommy is snoring softly on the air mattress, I lie awake in the dark, remembering each discovery. Each adventure. But my mind keeps drifting back to Discovery #77—the pipevine swallowtail butterfly.

Actually, it was a pipevine swallowtail *chrysalis*. When a caterpillar gets as big as it's going to get, it attaches itself to a branch or a leaf with a strand of silk, and its skin becomes a shell, and inside that shell the caterpillar transforms into a butterfly. While all this is happening, it's called a chrysalis.

We found the chrysalis in a tree in Tommy's backyard last fall. It was dangling from a branch like a strange Christmas ornament. I didn't think it was anything, but Tommy knew better. So for weeks, Tommy and I checked on that chrysalis every day after school. And every day, nothing happened. It just kept on dangling there.

Finally, we started seeing bright blue through the shell.

"Those are the wings," Tommy said.

The blue grew brighter, day after day . . .

. . . until, one afternoon, the chrysalis was gone.

We found the empty shell by the roots of the tree. The butterfly had flown away. And even though I was happy for the butterfly, seeing that broken shell made me sad. Because checking on that chrysalis every day . . . well, I'd gotten used to it. It had become part of my life, and suddenly it wasn't anymore. Suddenly things had changed.

I felt the same way when Mom first told me about Papa's Alzheimer's, and when I found out that Tommy was moving, and when Zoe was taken away to Emerald Springs.

I feel it again tonight.

This whole summer has been like that chrysalis, actually.

It crept by without me even noticing, until one day—today—it was almost gone.

I grab my watch from my nightstand and set an alarm for eight a.m. No, seven a.m. Because if tomorrow can't last forever, we should at least get an early start.

THIRTY-SEVEN

The morning sun beats down. Heat shimmers on the road and scorches my bare feet, and I know the day is only going to get hotter from here.

But there's a nice breeze, and it only smells a little bit like stinky fish. Even better, there are lots of animals out and about. Tommy and I spot a brown rabbit (Discovery #4) hopping through a neighbor's yard and a yellow-throated warbler (Discovery #35) on the eaves of a roof, singing a morning song. When I sit by the canal and dangle my feet in the water, tiny tadpoles (Discovery #12) dart around my toes.

None of these are new discoveries, but it still feels weird that we didn't bring the Discovery Journal with us. That even if we *did* make a discovery, we're all out of pages.

Before we saw the barn owl, we were planning on spending today trying to find our hundredth discovery. Now we don't know what to do.

"I hope Zoe shows up so you can tell her bye," I say.

"She can't know that today's my last day in Florida," Tommy says. He's standing behind me, keeping his distance from the water. "It would be irrational to expect to see her."

"Where d'you think she goes when she's not in the canal?"

"Into the river, probably."

I shade my eyes and look toward the far end of the canal, where it takes a turn behind Tommy's old house and feeds into the Indigo River. That's when I get a genius idea.

"Why wait for Zoe to come to us?" I say, standing up because genius ideas sound more genius-y when you're standing. "Why don't we go to her?"

"What are you suggesting, Peter?"

"Come on!" I say, grabbing his hand.

We run the length of the canal until we arrive panting on the doorstep of Tommy's old house. I give the door a few good knocks—not too loud, but not too soft, either.

"Peter, there's a 99.99 percent chance that this is a bad—" Tommy begins, but the door is already opening, and there's Mr. Reilly, wearing pajamas covered in little sailboats. His straw-colored hair pokes out at funny angles and his eyes are heavy with sleep. Or maybe a lack of sleep. He squints down at us while he slurps coffee from an Indigo River Boating Club mug.

It's really weird seeing Mr. Reilly answer Tommy's door, especially in pajamas. And I know it must be even weirder for Tommy. But I don't let the weirdness get me down.

"Good morning," I say, trying to find the right balance between calm and confident, like Maria Liu at the boating club meeting. Like my knock—not too loud, not too soft.

Mr. Reilly ignores me and frowns at Tommy. "You know you don't live here anymore, don't you?"

"Y-Yes, sir," says Tommy. "I'm visiting Peter."

"It's Tommy's last day here, actually," I say, "and we were wondering if we could borrow your canoe for the morning."

"My what?" Mr. Reilly says.

"His *what*?" Tommy says.

I point at the shiny red canoe sitting in the grass down by the dock.

Mr. Reilly's jaw clicks. "Don't know where that came from. Must be the neighbor's."

"Are you sure?" I say. "Because Mrs. Reilly said she bought it for you after Zoe was injured so you'd maybe not use your motorboat so much."

Mr. Reilly blinks. "You spoke to Elaine?"

"She came to watch Zoe's release."

258

"Was she . . . Is she . . ." He clears his throat. Well, he tries. "Did she say anything? About me?"

I'm not sure how to answer. I look at Tommy. He squirms. I give him my way-to-be-helpful look, then decide to tell Mr. Reilly the truth. I've been telling the truth a lot lately, and I'm getting pretty good at it.

"She said she hopes you're happy."

Mr. Reilly's shoulders slump. Coffee sloshes out of his mug. For a second his face looks a little softer—a little younger, too.

Then his scowl returns. He takes another noisy slurp of coffee and squints at Tommy. "Your parents didn't mention the leaky pipe in the upstairs bathroom."

"But, sir, there weren't any leaky pipes when we left."

"This house needs all kinds of work," he says. "I got swindled."

Okay, I *know* Tommy's parents, and they aren't swindlers. If there's a leaky pipe, it's probably because Mr. Reilly did something dumb and broke it. Or he's lying, the way he lied about not having a canoe.

I'm about to defend the honor of Mr. and Mrs. Saunders, but then I look beyond Mr. Reilly, at a living room full of unopened moving boxes. There's a bare mattress on the floor surrounded by lots of take-out food containers. I see the air hockey table, too. I wonder who he plays with now.

I close my eyes for a few seconds. When I open them, I

pretend I'm meeting Mr. Reilly for the first time. I pretend we've never been archnemeses. He could be anyone—even a not-completely-horrible person.

"My mom knows lots of repair people," I say. "Maybe she could recommend a plumber."

Mr. Reilly sneers, but it fades fast, like he can't hold on to it. "Take the canoe," he says. "And don't bring it back. What kind of boating club president would I be if I went around in a canoe?"

One who likes canoes, I think, but I don't say it, because I'm working on thinking more before I speak. I'm working on so much these days.

Mr. Reilly slams the door, then reopens it just a crack. "Get that plumber recommendation, will you?"

"Sure thing, Mr. Reilly."

The door shuts again, a little gentler this time. I look at Tommy. "People are weird," I say. "Aren't people weird?"

"Peter," he says, "I *can't* go in the river."

"You don't have to go *in* the river, Fox. We'll be in the canoe, high and dry."

"But how do you know we won't fall in? And what if we drift too far? And what if we get swept right out to sea?"

"Fox, don't you trust me?"

He wiggles and fidgets and I'm pretty sure he's about to say, *No, I don't trust you, Peter,* which would be pretty mean after everything we've been through.

But then he says, "Yes. Mostly. Like . . . eighty-seven percent."

I grin. "Good enough for me!"

We find a pair of life jackets in the canoe and strap them on. Neon yellow for Tommy, ice-pop orange for me.

Even with a life jacket, though, Tommy refuses to step into the water, so I have to push the canoe—with him sitting in it—into the canal myself. It's hard work, especially because my arms are still sore from lifting Zoe yesterday. But it's a downhill slope, and eventually the canoe edges into the water. I hop in before it drifts too far from the bank.

I canoed a few times with Papa when I was younger, but it's been years. I must be a natural pro, though, because I only crash the canoe into Mr. Reilly's dock about seven times before I get it moving down the canal. It's all about the rhythm of the oar. As Tommy tells me about the different kinds of bacteria that live in the water and might kill us if we fall in, the canoe sails forward, out of the canal and into the wide-open Indigo River.

"Whoa," I say.

I've seen the Indigo River a million times before. Every day of my life, probably. But now that I'm actually *in* the river, it looks so much bigger. Waves rock the canoe and it's all Tommy and I can do to hold it steady. That's when Tommy makes a funny yelping sound, like Cassidy when she merges on the highway.

"You okay, Fox?"

"Define *okay*," he says.

Maybe keeping him busy will help. I hand him the second oar so he can row, too.

"I'll try," he says. "But you know I have weak arms. Which way?"

I look up and down the river. To the south, houses line the shore as far as the eye can see. There are some houses to the north, too, but not as many, and I know from my biking route that there's a lot more nature that way, which means there might be manatees, too. Plus, the river flows south, and we should go *against* the flow of the river now so it's easier to get back later when our arms are even more tired. That's smart thinking.

"North," I say, dipping my oar in the water and turning us to face upriver. Like I said, I'm a natural pro.

As we paddle, we keep an eye out for manatees. We see some fish and a floating mass of seaweed, but no big gray blobs. No Zoe.

"Maybe we shouldn't go *too* far from the canal," Tommy says. I hear the doubt creeping into his voice, like maybe he only trusts me 82 percent now instead of 87 percent.

I look behind us. "We *haven't* gone that far from the canal! We've barely moved at all. How is that possible?"

Suddenly a motorboat roars past us. We almost capsize in the waves it leaves in its wake, and that's when my genius idea starts to feel a little less genius-y. I'm sweating up a storm, for one thing. The sun feels even hotter on the river, and the only relief is when Tommy accidentally flings water at me with his oar, which happens a lot.

Also, Mom probably wouldn't be too happy if she knew we were out here. Before she left for work this morning, she told me and Tommy not to get into "too much trouble" while she was gone. This might just fall into the "too much trouble" category.

"I hate to say it, Fox, but . . . maybe we should turn back and just bike along the shore."

"Wait," Tommy says, lurching forward. "There!"

It takes me a few seconds to see it—the sun glares off the water, and sweat is stinging my eyes—but then I spy a shadow beneath the waves. A manatee-shaped shadow.

I'm so excited I almost drop my oar in the river. "Is it Zoe?"

"I don't think so," Tommy says. "This one looks smaller."

"Hey, where's it going?"

"It's over there. No, wait—I lost it."

We stop rowing so we don't accidentally hit the manatee with the oars. "We should really get polarized sunglasses," I say.

"It'll surface again," Tommy says.

So we wait, and drift, and hope, until the manatee

breaches again, just a few yards away. I catch a glimpse of the scar pattern on its back. There's no Z, and Tommy's right—this manatee is definitely smaller than Zoe.

When the manatee starts moving up the river, there's no more talk of turning back. No more yelps from Tommy, either. We just row, softly but quickly, keeping our eyes trained on the water so we can follow the shadow. The heat doesn't feel so suffocating anymore. My arms don't feel so sore, either. I feel like I could row for days and days.

Eventually the manatee swims into a shallow area where the shore bends like a crescent moon around the river. I set down my oar and rub my stinging eyes. When I open them again, I don't see the manatee. "Where'd it go?"

"Over there," Tommy says, pointing.

"Wait," I say. "No, it's over *there*."

"I think that's a different manatee."

"Is *that* one Zoe?"

"I can't tell," says Tommy.

We row toward the second manatee, barely dipping the oars into the water, and that's when I realize that there aren't just two manatees. There are three—no, four—no, too many to count. They're *everywhere*.

My skin prickles and my heart swells as I look at the curving shore. It's lined with lots of palms and thick bushes. That must be why this area doesn't look familiar—the biking trail is on the other side of those trees. I wouldn't really be able to see the river from over there.

"Fox," I say, breathless, "would you call this a cove?"

"It curves into the land," says Tommy. "I think that makes it a cove."

For a second I don't know if I'm going to start laughing or crying, and then I start laughing *and* crying.

"Um, Peter, are you okay?"

I nod as I watch the manatees—all different sizes, all different scar patterns—rising and sinking and swirling around the canoe.

Then I take off my life jacket and shirt and shoes and solar system watch.

"Peter," says Tommy, trying to hold the boat steady, "what are you doing?"

I wiggle my toes. Tears tickle my cheeks. "Getting a closer look," I say.

"But, Peter, the bacteria!"

The canoe rocks beneath me as I slip over the side and into the Indigo River. The water isn't very cold, but it still feels like heaven after sweating buckets all morning. It doesn't take long for something rubbery to brush against my leg, then my arm. Laughter bubbles up inside me like fizzy soda.

"Be careful!" Tommy says. "Stay close to the canoe, and if you feel a current, remember—"

I don't know what else Tommy says, because I dunk my

head under the river and my world turns to water.

I can't see very far, but through a haze of algae and bubbles, there are the manatees—gray giants floating all around me, nudging me gently as they munch on the dancing grass along the riverbed. I swim between them until my lungs ache.

When I come up for air, Tommy is still going.

"—swimming is really tiring and sometimes you don't even notice it. You have to be careful not to exhaust yourself—"

"Wanna join me?"

Tommy looks at me like I just suggested he chug a gallon of Indigo River bacteria. "You know I can't."

"Rivers don't have rip currents, Fox."

"I'm wearing glasses."

"You can take off glasses, you know."

"I'm legally blind without them, and I can't— So I'll just— I'm going to stay in the canoe."

I almost tell him to stop being so afraid, but I know it took a lot of courage for him to get in that canoe with me—not to mention the courage it took to hop a plane from Michigan just to see me again.

"Sure," I say. "Just give me a minute, okay?"

I dive underwater again and take a closer look at the patterns on the manatees' backs. They've all been struck by boats. Most of them have probably been struck by several. I don't see any Zs, though. Where is she? She's got to be here. I know it. I can *feel* it.

A rush of bubbles clouds my vision. I turn and see Tommy bobbing in the water beside me, his cheeks puffed out and his eyes pinched shut, his legs kicking as fast as propellers. He even took his life jacket off. I grab his arm and tug him to the surface.

"Fox! You're in the water! What changed your mind?"

"I'm being brave," he splutters. "This is me being brave."

"Super brave," I say. "Definitely in the bravest subset of human beings."

"Really?"

"Really. But . . . maybe try not to kick so much around the manatees."

"I don't want to sink."

"Tommy, you *know* how to swim."

"I know, it's just—"

"I've got you," I say, squeezing his arm.

His legs slow down and the water settles, but when he looks around, panic creeps back into his voice. "Where's the canoe?"

"The river's pushing it toward the shore," I say. "We should beach it, just in case. Come on!"

I guide Tommy toward the canoe, weaving carefully

through the herd of manatees. After we push the boat onto the shore, we sit beside it for a minute, catching our breath. The sun is higher in the sky now and the heat feels good after our swim. I let it warm my skin while we watch the manatees, trying to count them all.

"Fifteen?" says Tommy.

"What? There are at *least* twenty."

"Whoa," he says.

"Whoa," I agree. "Up for another swim?"

"Okay. But you have to hold my hand."

"Duh!"

We run back into the water, Tommy's hand tangled up with mine, but we stop when we spot a turtle perched on a rock in the shallows. "Hey, look," I say. "Discovery #19!"

Tommy hunches over for a closer look. "Discovery #19 was a river cooter turtle. This one is different. See that red stripe on its back? And the bottom of its shell is orange. Peter, I think this is a new discovery."

"But we don't have any more room in the journal!"

"Scientists think there are 8.7 million species on Earth," Tommy says. "So we couldn't possibly have gotten them all in one journal."

"8.7 *million*?"

"That's just an estimate. The actual number could be much higher."

I try to process 8.7 million—I try to see the number in

my head—but I can't. It's just too much. And I know that even if I spend the rest of my life searching for animals, I'll never discover and draw all 8.7 million. I'm a real discovery pro, but that's just impossible.

Suddenly, standing here with Tommy in the Indigo River, the world feels so big. Scary big. My chest tightens, and the weight of all the things that I don't know—that I might *never* know—just about flattens me.

Tomorrow morning Mom and I will drive Tommy to the airport so he can go back to Michigan. A few days later, I'll start middle school. I don't know if I'll like my new school or if I'll make new friends. I don't know when I'll see Tommy again. I don't know who will keep the finished Discovery Journal.

I don't know what's going to happen to Papa, either. I don't know when he'll come home, or if his dementia will ever get better, or when he'll get to meet Zoe.

I don't know if Mom will sell enough houses that Mr. Reilly doesn't own and become Space Coast Real Estate Agent of the Year again.

I don't know if the Indigo River Boating Club will start trying to protect manatees.

I don't even know if Cassidy and Billy will end up together!

My mind is a Category 5 hurricane, thoughts and questions swirling around like mad, and I'm pretty sure this is it—this is the moment I finally explode.

But I don't. I remind myself to breathe—big inhale, big exhale. I dig my toes deeper into the mushy seaweed beneath my feet and feel the sun toasting my skin. I crinkle my nose as a fishy breeze whooshes past us. I listen to the *quack* of ducks flying above us and the *ribbit* of frogs coming from the reeds along the bank.

"Peter?" Tommy says.

"Come on, Fox," I say.

We splash our way back into the river, and this time, when we dive underwater, Tommy keeps his eyes open. I know he can't see very well without his glasses, but he doesn't need to see far. The manatees are right in front of us, beside us, behind us. Everywhere we look, we see manatees. We hang between them all, suspended in the water, holding our breath for as long as we possibly can.

When we surface, Tommy says, "Hey, Peter? This might be the best day ever. I can't say for sure. I can't remember every day I've ever lived, and I don't know what all the days in the future will be like, but . . ." He smiles. I really like his smile. "The best day ever."

Then the best day ever gets better. Because on our next dive, I make another discovery. It's not a new discovery, but it's still the greatest. Through the pack of manatees, a familiar face swims toward us. I recognize her before I even see the Z on her back.

She must recognize me, too, because she swims so close that we're face-to-face, eye to beady eye. I know not to touch her—"Respect All Wildlife" is the most important rule of the Discovery Club.

But then she lowers her head and pushes her snout against my chest, right against my beating heart.

I squeeze Tommy's hand. He squeezes mine back.

The other manatees dance around us, glittering in the sunlight, and Zoe stays right here, snout to chest.

Just wait till Papa hears about this.

AUTHOR'S NOTE

Like Peter, I grew up in central Florida where the storms come sudden and strong and the summer heat can steal your breath away. Peter's neighborhood is based on my own. Sometimes, sitting on the grassy bank of the canal that ran through my neighborhood, I was lucky enough to spot manatees in the water.

I didn't realize at the time that the West Indian manatee was unique to my corner of the country. Later, when life carried me away from Florida, these gentle gray giants continued to swim dreamlike through my imagination. I remained enchanted by them, so years later I returned to Florida to learn more about them.

During my visit, I swam with manatees in the Crystal River, visited manatee rehabilitation centers, and talked to manatee experts. Emerald Springs State Park is fictional, but it was inspired by a visit to Homosassa Springs Wildlife State Park, home to a variety of animals, including manatees, that—for different reasons—are unable to live in the wild.

As Peter and Tommy learn, the survival of the West Indian manatee is a testament to the work of generations of heroic manatee conservationists. But Florida manatees continue to face many threats, from boating strikes to warming waters caused by climate change. The conservation work is ongoing. At the time of this writing, manatees in the Indian River Lagoon—a highly biodiverse estuary that inspired the fictional Indigo River—are struggling to find enough food because human pollution has caused widespread destruction of the sea grass that manatees eat.

While the Florida Manatee Society and the Florida Marine Life Commission are organizations of my own invention, there are real organizations fighting to protect manatees and their habitats, including the Save the Manatee Club. To learn more about this club's critical work and to get involved, visit www.savethemanatee.org. And if there's another animal that you love, a little research will likely reveal organizations devoted to protecting it, especially if the animal is vulnerable to extinction.

As Peter argues in his speech to the Indigo River Boating Club, we have the responsibility—and the joy—of being caretakers for the natural world and all the amazing creatures that call it home.

ACKNOWLEDGMENTS

This book began as a short story that I wrote during my time at the Writing for Children and Young Adults program at Vermont College of Fine Arts (VCFA). I am indebted to my faculty adviser at the time, Mary Quattlebaum, who suggested that I turn the short story into a novel—and then kindly but firmly asked, "How is your manatee novel going?" every time I saw her. These nudges were inspiring! Thank you to faculty adviser David Gill, as well, for offering guidance on the early pages.

The entire VCFA community is an endless source of support and encouragement. There are too many wonderful people to name, but I do want to give a shout-out to my classmates-turned-critique-partners Tanya Aydelott, Adina Baseler, and Emma Powers. Thank you for being my companions on this journey. Your minds and hearts are brilliant.

Speaking of brilliant minds and hearts: Michael Bourret, you rock. Thank you for believing in this story, advocating for it, and finding it a loving home. The superstar editorial team at Quill Tree—Andrew Eliopulos, Karen Chaplin, Celina Sun, Rosemary Brosnan—guided this story deftly and lovingly. I'm deeply grateful to everyone else at Harper who laid a hand on this book along the way: Alexandra Rakaczki and Jen Strada in managing editorial and copy-editing, Laura Mock and David Curtis in design, Sean Cavanagh and Vanessa Nuttry in production, Emma Meyer in marketing, Jacquelynn Burke in publicity, and Andrea Pappenheimer and her team in sales. You are all my heroes.

My thanks and admiration to Paddy Donnelly for the gorgeous cover art. It makes my heart sing. (If you aren't already familiar with the rest of his work, check it out! It's incredible.)

Gratitude and love to my family—Mom, Dad, Chris—for supporting my storytelling obsession since I was old enough to talk and for bearing with me as I mined aspects of my childhood and fictionalized them in order to write *Manatee Summer.*

And finally, a sea-cow-sized thank-you to manatees for being a source of delight and wonder. It's so cool to share this planet with you.